New Tal

The knife slashed downw

And even as it did, t

How can I explain it? You switch off an electric fire, the elements slowly darken; you turn off the current to a valve radio, but you still hear the sound for a few seconds.

So they—spirits, ghosts, revenants, whatever they were—became wraith-like, dimmed and dwindled.

In five seconds they had disappeared, and there was nothing left in the room.

Nothing except the old-fashioned operating table, and the body on it, and the blood dripping from the great gashes in its throat.

Also edited by Hugh Lamb
in Magnum Books

FORGOTTEN TALES OF TERROR

New Tales of Terror

edited by
HUGH LAMB

MAGNUM BOOKS
Methuen Paperbacks Ltd

A Magnum Book

NEW TALES OF TERROR
ISBN 0 417 05690 7

First published in Great Britain 1980
by Magnum Books

Magnum Books are published
by Methuen Paperbacks Ltd
11 New Fetter Lane, London EC4P 4EE

Made and printed in Great Britain
by Richard Clay (The Chaucer Press) Ltd
Bungay, Suffolk

This one is for S.A.M.

Acknowledgements

I am extremely grateful to certain of the authors in here who replied to a request for stories with some of the best material to come my way for a long time. Individual acknowledgements are due to: Robert Haining, for *Sylow Springs*; Ken Dickson, for *The Snorkel, the Starfish and the Salt, Salt Sea*; Elizabeth Fancett, for *A Strange and Awful Coincidence* and *Baby Hate*; Brian Lumley, for *Snarker's Son*; Rosemary Timperley and Harvey Unna and Stephen Durbridge Ltd, for *Some Travellers Return*; Ken Alden, for *Justice Tresilian in the Tower*; Les Freeman, for *Mind*; T. H. McCormick, for *Morton*; Eleanor Inglefield, for *The Singing Stream*; Adrian Cole, for *Midnight Hag*; and Robert Aickman, for *The Fetch*.

Contents

Introduction

AFTER A SELECTION OF FORGOTTEN TALES of terror in my last Magnum book, I am very pleased to present some original stories. I hope NEW TALES OF TERROR will prove to be as entertaining—and as frightening—as its predecessor. The authors have done their best to ensure just that.

We start with a writer who I regard as one of the leading talents in this field to emerge in the past decade—Robert Haining. Readers of my anthologies will be familiar with his remarkable talent and those about to sample his work for the first time are in for a pleasant surprise. Robert (the brother of noted anthologist Peter Haining) is a university lecturer who worked in America and Northern Ireland before his present post at Sheffield University. I count myself fortunate in being the first editor to use a Robert Haining story, back in 1975. Since then he has produced several fine tales and in 1979, published his first novel THE SOUL EATER, written in collaboration with Mike Legat. *Sylow Springs* draws on Robert's American sojourn and will sharpen your palate for the savoury items to follow. But give it careful attention—it will also sharpen your wits . . .

Our next contributor, Ken Dickson, is here making his debut in a book. Born in Edinburgh, Ken now lives in Wiltshire, where he works for the Post Office in, as he puts it, "a vaguely executive capacity". You are at liberty to guess what. Ken's association with the macabre is of long standing; at the time of writing he is secretary of the British Fantasy Society. Although he has been writing for some time, his stories have previously only appeared in small circulation magazines and it is about time he saw the light of print in a book. Not the least entertaining aspect of *The Snorkel, The Starfish and the Salt, Salt Sea* is the title. There are, however, some interesting things in the story itself, as you will discover.

Then we have the first of two short but telling items from Elizabeth Fancett, one of our most prolific writers in this field. Listeners to Capital Radio's MOMENT OF TERROR series will know her work of old; for those outside the London area, this is a series of five-minute horror tales broadcast late at night. Miss Fancett has contributed over 70 stories to the series. Elizabeth Fancett's interest in horror and science fiction started in 1966, when she submitted a story to the BBC's late-night horror series. She could already claim a long career as a free-lance journalist and film critic; the success of her first horror story led her to concentrate on this field. She has appeared in every major horror anthology series in Britain, has been published all over Europe and has had some of her stories broadcast on Israeli Radio. She hopes to publish her first collection of science-fiction stories shortly. Our two Elizabeth Fancett tales concern a man lost in a cave who meets another soul in the same plight, and a father who thinks his baby son does not like him. Miss Fancett is not one for too many happy endings.

In lighter tone (in parts, that is) comes *Snarker's Son*, a science-fiction romp from Brian Lumley, now established as one of the leading British horror writers. Brian, who hails from County Durham, began his writing career with some notable pastiches of H. P. Lovecraft, which caught the attention of August Derleth. Arkham House, Derleth's publishing imprint, has issued several of Brian's books in the past few years and he has gained a wide reputation both here and in America. It is gratifying to report that Brian has successfully produced many good stories outside the Lovecraft milieu, and here is one of them.

Snarker's Son contains many surprises, one of which is the Tubers. Fear not, you will learn all about *them* . . .

Some Travellers Return by Rosemary Timperley is a finely wrought piece of haunting simplicity, as we would expect from Britain's leading female horror writer. Rosemary has been in the business since the early 1950s and has contributed to all the major horror and ghost story collections, as well as editing a good few herself. Like Elizabeth Fancett, she has also been well represented in the MOMENT OF TERROR series. In addition to her short story work, Rosemary Timperley has produced over 40 novels. She knows just how to get the reader on the hook—and when to pull in the line.

After Rosemary Timperley, quite the strangest story in the book. Three years ago, I presented a first story by a young West Country writer, Ken Alden. It was a most original story, one of a batch of manuscripts he sent me. Mr Alden is not short of ideas—the rest of those manuscripts contained stories built around such novel notions as Freud and Jung debating sex and the supernatural, and a ghost story set in Boleskine House, Aleister Crowley's old (pardon the pun) haunt on the shores of Loch Ness. In the story I used, Ken Alden had spent much time translating Latin from the period to give his characters authenticity. He also said at the time that he had finished three long novels but had not typed them out. Mr Alden takes his work seriously. *Justice Tresilian in the Tower* is unique. I've never read anything like it myself, and I don't think you will have either. It blends such disparate elements as the Tower of London, Wat Tyler's revolt, Richard the Second, an ancient British god and ley lines into something very special.

From historical London we move to present-day Whitby, in Les Freeman's story *Mind*. This is only the second appearance of a work of fiction by Mr Freeman, but he is no stranger to print. A career spanning 20 years in journalism has seen him contributing to such newspapers as the *Daily Express*, the *Birmingham Post* and *The Northern Echo*; he is at present the editor of *Water*. In his spare time, Les Freeman writes plays and poetry, and now is turning his hand to fiction. I mentioned

Whitby above, because Les knows this part of the country well, and it is not the first time that this Yorkshire town has featured in a tale of terror. You'll recall that Dracula spent a memorable vacation there. However, the horrors in *Mind* are not anything so mundane as vampirism; on the contrary, this is a well thought out and executed study in psychic terror, on a most original theme.

T. H. McCormick's *Morton*, meanwhile, goes even further north, to Scotland, for the background of its hero and villain. And quite right, too, for this is a tale from a writer Glasgow-born and bred who still lives there. Mr McCormick progressed from journalism to short-story writing some years ago and has already appeared in the PAN HORROR series, as well as the London *Evening News*, *Weekend*, *Titbits*, *Knave* and *Penthouse*. He maintains that most of his published stories have been crime fiction, from a light humorous angle, but horror stories are dearest to his heart. This tale must have been very close to his aorta, in that case; it is exceedingly grim.

Much, much gentler, I promise you, is Eleanor Inglefield's *The Singing Stream*, a new story from a charming writer. Miss Inglefield is a niece of Frederick Delius and a long-standing resident of that magical county, Cornwall. Eleanor Inglefield has been writing about Cornwall for many years, contributing articles and stories for West Country magazines and newspapers. Three years ago, I introduced her story *The Music in the House*, a blend of charm and terror. *The Singing Stream* is composed of the same elements and is based on genuine Cornish legend. It will stay in the mind a long time after reading.

Adrian Cole also sets his story in the West Country, as befits a writer born in Plymouth and now resident in Bideford. But unlike Miss Inglefield, his tale is pure terror, and worthy of careful attention. Adrian Cole has been writing full-time for just a few years but already he has established himself on both sides of the Atlantic as a contender for the highest honours this rather restricted field can bestow. He writes in several veins—

horror and science fiction (both blended in his two novels MADNESS EMERGING and PATHS IN DARKNESS), sheer fantasy (as in his Dream Lords trilogy PLAGUE OF NIGHTMARES, LORD OF NIGHTMARES and BANE OF NIGHTMARES) and humour (he has entertained audiences at the British Fantasy Society convention with some of this and I have seen the stolidest horror enthusiasts literally rolling in the aisles as a result). Alas, there's no humour in *Midnight Hag*. Instead this is a nasty little story of supernatural terror with a closing scene second to none.

And to close the book, a new long story from our finest writer of ghost stories and supernatural fantasy, Robert Aickman. There have been so many superlatives bestowed on this gentleman's ghost stories that it is hard to find anything new to say. His first forays into this field came nearly 30 years ago with a book entitled WE ARE FOR THE DARK, written jointly with Elizabeth Jane Howard. Since then, through five collections of his own stories and eight skilled selections of other authors, to my mind he has maintained his position as our best weaver of tales of terror. Where other writers merely frighten, Aickman enchants and frightens with stories that are real literature. There could be no finer closing work to this concert of fear than a new work by Robert Aickman. *The Fetch* awaits you.

If you enjoy these stories as much as I enjoyed picking them out, then you'll be well pleased. And that's enough from me—you're on your own from here on.

Hugh Lamb
SUTTON, SURREY

Robert Haining

SYLOW SPRINGS

JUST AS THE SUN STARTED TO sink below the ridge of barren hills, turning the winter sun into thin streams of cold piercing light, Sam turned his car off the tollway and on to the exit road for Sylow Springs. The journey was nearly over. Three weeks travelling in Montana and North Dakota had come to an end and he could look forward to a well-earned rest—and he needed it! Every mile from Rapid City to Missoula had ached in his bones. He had driven it partly at night when all he could see were the glaring lights of oncoming cars and the drab neon signs of seedy motels and cheap eating houses. But then, as he well knew, that was the best time for US 10. He had driven it so often he could picture every mile of it in his mind's eye.

Every time he had come out West it had been the same old story of endless days travelling the highways and interstates of the North-West, trying to sell what seemed in this place the unsellable. That made it all the worse so that after a few days he would become homesick. Then the rest of the assignment would drag by as this one had done—cheerless empty days following long cold nights. At least this trip was over. Sam paused at a quiet intersection and reminded himself that there would be others. He sighed and pushed back his hat. Yes, there would always be another chance to see all those places again.

Sam parked the station wagon in Main Street and slid it out of gear. He took his hat off and tossed it on to the seat beside him and then pulled himself out of the car for a good stretch. The long drive had not helped the digestion of the worst meal he had had all trip and he felt sick as he stood in the fading sunlight and looked around him at the heart of the old town.

Was it because he always finished his trips here, or was there something in the air? He did not like Sylow Springs—it made him think of depression years, the ones his father used to talk about. His father had been steeped in the depression from his ugly flat black shoes to his faded check shirt that he wore with the sleeves rolled. Sylow Springs seemed to be a barely living reminder of all that. His father would have liked it here, the sense of mouldering poverty would have suited him.

It's just beneath the surface, Sam, the poverty I mean. It's like a cancer. It eats away and it gets you in the end. It eats through the surface, Sam, even when you think everything is fine. Poverty's always there. You remember that.

So here was where the cancer showed through, where things rotted. No one bothered to cover anything up, it was all left on display.

Sam cast his eye down Main Street. It was late afternoon, but not so late that there could not be a few signs of activity. Yet the place seemed almost deserted. He wanted a restaurant where he could get warm and get rid of the taste of that pizza. "Ed's" was open, he could see it over the road, a large red neon light cutting the line of boarded tenements. Sam wandered over to get something to eat.

How often had he seen such a place before? He pushed the door open to the smell of frying bacon and the line of polished formica. How often had he seen and smelt it all before—the old men leaning over the counter, the smell of strong coffee that could help you put another two hundred miles on the clock? It was another meal in another seedy restaurant. Even the man behind the counter was the same, with the same white apron and tired expression. Perhaps it was Ed himself? Sam had often thought that he would like to find out some time how many places were really run by the little men whose names always appeared on the signboards. In the meantime he would have something to eat; black coffee first and then a steak and fries.

"Oh, and a salad too, Ed." The eyes were dead and the face like putty. Nothing reacted, so perhaps this was one against the tally.

The tired old men at the far end of the table seemed to stir momentarily as his voice carried across the rows of empty seats. They seemed put out by his presence and cast occasional glances in his direction. Sam could feel their hostility and read their thoughts that seemed etched on their ill, uncared-for faces and their worn, faded clothing. The balance had been upset, their late afternoon sanctuary invaded, and they were weighing him up, like his father used to do sitting at the breakfast table when he was late for work.

Think you're pretty fine in a new suit of clothes. Nothing lasts. It's only the surface and the surface rots easy. Then you find out how it really is. When the finery has gone. When everything has been sucked out. That's when you find out how easy everything just falls away.

Sam ate and left. He could do without old men's faces reminding him of what was stalking him—what had always stalked him. His father had been good at that. Even when he had got his first job and brought home his first pay packet, his father had been there to say: *And mind you stick it. When they lay people off, it's the last in that gets the sign. You stick it and then maybe you won't be the first.*

So Sam had stuck the job until his back ached and he had finally been promoted. He became a salesman but even then his father had been around to say: *They don't need salesmen when the depression comes. There's nothing to sell. Then how will you keep your house, your car? Who'll feed your wife and kids then? It always comes, don't fool yourself. Then you find out how it really is. All this is surface. It's nothing.*

Across the street, the travel office was still open. A young girl came to one of the windows and started to pull the curtains. Sam stopped to look at her. She had pretty legs and a bright fresh face. She threw him a smile as she disappeared into the darkness of the front office and Sam followed her, in through the front door.

"Can I help you, sir?"

Sam saw her at one of the counters. There were four but only one was open. She was standing looking at him, but he could not see her legs.

"I want a ticket," he said and walked over to her. "I want a plane ticket to Chicago."

"Yes, sir, when are you leaving?"

Sam had not thought too clearly about that but he wanted to go as soon as he could.

"Today's flight has gone. It leaves mid-afternoon. If you like, I can book you on tomorrow's."

Sam cursed his luck. It meant nearly a day in Sylow Springs and that was just about the last thing he had wanted.

"I can route you via Madison for a little extra? That flight leaves this evening."

And there was his father again, looking over his shoulder and whispering in his ear: *You can't afford to go paying extra. You've got a wife and children to support. You'll need every cent you've got. It may look good now, but it's coming. You save that money, find a cheap hotel and save the money.*

Sam looked at her for the first time. He was disappointed. The pretty smile, the pretty face had not been there before she had reached for her make-up box. She was not so young either. That was the trouble, sometimes his father was right.

"No, that's fine, I'll wait till tomorrow. Book me on the direct flight."

Sam took his ticket out on to the street and stood in the light of a street lamp as he fitted it into his top pocket. The sun had set and what little had been going on in Sylow Springs was slowly coming to an end. The best plan was to find an hotel. He needed some sleep and would not mind where he stayed. Sam strolled back to his car. He knew of a cheap hotel which he had gone to often in the past. It was the sort of hotel that his father would have approved of.

No need to go wasting your money, son.

Sam drove the big estate wagon down Main Street, past the lines of drinking houses and dime stores. Was that all a man could find to do when he was laid off? Sam could not imagine what it would be like to be in Sylow Springs without a job. He hated the place enough as it was. But what was left of a man who lived his life in Sylow Springs and then lost his job? Where would he go, what would he do if the unthinkable were to happen?

A large green sedan cruised past him and after that a police car. The policeman in the driving seat looked at him. He had seen the out-of-state licence and had decided he had better take a look at who was in the car. He was probably paid by the local mining company to keep an eye out for reporters. Since the vein had started petering out, the company had had to lay off men and cut corners on safety just to stay profitable. They did not like reporters to get too close to the mines, taking pictures and asking questions. They particularly did not like pictures. The one smelter just out of town had been working all day every day covering the town in a thin yellowish dust. It made the eyes sting and the nose run. Anyone taking pictures was liable to be told he was on company property. Then the simplest way out was to give up your camera. It was all the same to the policeman. There was no need for trouble.

On the left at the intersection was the old movie theatre. It had closed since Sam's last visit and with it the restaurant next door. Sam wondered if the hotel would be open, but he need not have worried. Places like the Grand Hotel do not close down. Sometimes they fall down, occasionally they are pulled down, but no one would pull down the Grand Hotel. It was too precious a reminder of that golden age of Sylow Springs when everything had been—dependable. The Grand was left because it was one of the few buildings that from the outside at least could help you to picture what Sylow Springs had once been—a big, prosperous, bustling mining town.

Sylow Springs had been built on tin and the mine barons had come and had sucked the metal like greedy children sucking orange through a straw. They had come and they had dug their mines and they had built their factories and they had built their palaces. Most of all, they had valued their palaces—their homes, their fine restaurants, their fine hotels like the Grand and their symbols of civic dignity. Allan J. Mc Crompton on his stony pedestal by the steps of City Hall kept a watchful eye on the mines, the factories and most of all the miners themselves. Order and discipline had been his watchwords and now on the steps of the city hall he had given to the people a visual reminder, a personification, of those two foremost virtues. He it was who had crushed the miners' strike of 1919 and it was his money that had raised up City Hall. It was fitting then that the man who had made Sylow Springs safe for the mine barons should be a symbol of their era.

Yet that is all ancient history. Since those days the tin has gone thin and the barons have mostly drifted away, taking their profits and leaving Sylow Springs to a slow death. Now the town is run by the few who remain. It is a decaying rotting shell and nothing attests more eloquently to that decline than the Grand Hotel.

The Grand had seen many changes and all of them for the worst. It had suffered a loss of status. From the elegant hotel it first was, it became more middle class. The trappings had all been retained but they had that unpleasant tinge about them. They were used, slightly stained, slightly worn. Still genteel and quite romantic, it was definitely not for those of impeccable taste or limitless financial resources. But in time even the middle classes had felt bound to avoid it. It became seedy. At first it was seedy but in a fairly genteel way, so that at first sight the weary traveller, unfamiliar to Sylow Springs, might have been forgiven for choosing it as a night's rest. Sadly, he would soon discover that the wardrobes were dirty and tattered, the carpets worn. He would discover a nameless and slightly distasteful aroma in the vicinity of the toilets. It was a little seedy and the traveller would note not to return should he ever have the misfortune to be in Sylow Springs again.

Then time continued its inevitable forward progression so that its seediness became unmistakable. New laws required safety ladders. In the absence of more money, or better taste, the hideous ironmongery was allowed to cascade down the front of the building, obliterating the elegant stone facade. On the inside, the gradual decay was now apparent for all to see. No one could pass the entrance without sensing that unmistakable odour of poverty and slow inevitable collapse. Now it became the stopping place for the poorer folk, the poor factory worker, the poor mine worker. To attract its new clientele, the Grand had had to erect a neon sign. Yet by the time Sam came to it, pulling his station wagon to a halt in its deserted and unlit parking lot, even this vestige of respectability had been eroded. The Grand was now nothing more than the resting place of pimps and prostitutes, vagrants and criminals. The kind of place you hide out in if you want to keep your movements undercover. A fairly elegant hiding place, true, but none the less more a shelter than a home.

Sam got out of the car and took his case with him up the broad front steps and through the elegant revolving doors. The grand and spacious lobby seemed just a little drabber than it had been on the last occasion. Two or three cigarette machines had gone up and there was even a small potted plant on one of the tables, but on the other hand two of the chandeliers had gone, a section of panelling had been torn off and the armchairs had been removed. The musty smell was perhaps a little stronger.

"Room for the night?"

Sam was addressing a small man who sat with his feet up behind the desk, ticking something off in his newspaper. The clerk did not look up. Why should he bother? The Grand was the type of hotel that if you were the sort who came seeking a room you could not be the sort worth looking up for. The man pointed to a pile of registration cards.

"Fill in the card, mister." Every word came flat and dull.

Sam filled in the card and all the while the man carried on ticking the newspaper columns. When Sam had finished he waited for his key. Behind the clerk were rows of pigeon holes each containing a key. Only one short row was empty. Sam remembered that it was the same row as last time. Did the clerk put everyone together in the same place so it felt more homey or because that was the only inhabitable part? For a moment he felt an overwhelming urge to leave. The seediness, the atmosphere of grand elegance in a state of inexorable and cloying decay nauseated his senses. The hotel was like a powdered elegant old lady trying hard to conceal her encroaching senility. The place reeked of death and its cosmetics. But if he had any doubts about staying his father soon reminded him.

It'll do, son.

The clerk flicked a key towards him. It slithered over the desk top and Sam grabbed it.

"Find your own way?" It was barely a question. Sam picked up his suitcase and walked up the short flight of stairs to the first landing.

Even by day the corridors were dark and dank, by evening the effect was even stronger, the smell of heavy disinfectant barely covering the heavier smell of mould. Sam tapped one of the wall lights which flickered on and off. He smiled to himself, almost satisfied by the familiarity of it all. It was just as he had remembered it. As he walked up the elegant spiral staircase, now worn and faded, he caught sight of the elevator cage out of order and suspended between two floors, just as it had been before.

His room was on the third floor and this part of the hotel seemed almost respectable. Perhaps bits of carpet and drape had been brought to this floor to at least give the appearance that attention was paid to the comforts of the guest. But the improvement was only on the surface. Behind the drapes, the walls were stained and the windows were grimy and broken. Sam peered through one down into a central courtyard piled with refuse. A man was turning over the rubbish and looked up as Sam peered down. He soon turned away, returning to his search.

The room itself was at the front of the building overlooking Main Street. He was next to the neon light which would add another measure of discomfort after dark to the city traffic and the general air of decay from which his own room was not exempt. Here, as elsewhere, the carpet was faded and mouldy, the furniture worn and ugly. Sam felt the bed, it was clean but badly sprung. Little if any of that former style survived to remind the guest of what the Grand had once been. Quietly and in the presence of just a handful of transients, yesterday's elegance was rotting as surely as those it had once adorned.

Sam lay down on the bed. He felt tired. In the distance a factory hooter sounded. He relaxed into the clean sheets. If he could sleep through until the morning, nothing would please him more. Sleep was the same wherever you were.

On a cold, clear, crisp November morning a plane burned on a ploughed field outside Chicago, Illinois. Sam knew because he was there. A short distance from where he was standing, Ellie was watching the burning wreck too. Next to her were their two sons.

"Ellie!"

Sam called over to her but she did not seem to hear him or see him. He tried waving but she refused to look at him.

It seemed strange to Sam that no one else was there except Ellie and the boys. There was no one helping the injured and no one trying to douse the flames which just seemed to grow taller and taller.

"Stand back, Ellie, it might blow."

Scattered around the plane were bodies. Everything seemed

so desperately quiet, so irrevocably still. Only the red tail light continued to revolve, splattering a blood-drenched light over the harsh unyielding landscape. Why had no one come to put out the flames and take away the dead? Why was Ellie here?

At his feet, a man lay face down in the mud. He tried to step over him to get to Ellie but the mud seemed to hold him. Ellie was turning away now, leading the boys away. At his feet a thin trail of blood from the dead man's head reached a pool of brown muddy water caught in between the ridges of the ploughed field. The blood spread out across the surface of the water, touching his shoes. Sam knelt down to the corpse and lifted the head.

"Ellie!"

Sam broke from his dream in a cold sweat. The room was quite black now and the first thing he was aware of was the flickering red neon light that sent ripples of colour across the ceiling and the far wall. The noise of thunder reached him. Out over the hills, storm clouds were gathering and pressing down on the town. Sam could see none of this but the air was noticeably heavier. He seemed wrapped in silence.

Sam reached for his coat and took out a pack of cigarettes. He lit one, drawing heavily on it and then stubbing it out on the ashtray. He let himself relax and then lay back. The face on the ploughed field had been his own, he had seen, smelt, touched his own death as one would a piece of meat on a butcher's slab. Ellie had been there, but it was as if nothing could be done. In any case, he reminded himself, he did not believe in premonitions of death. He reached out again for his packet of cigarettes and his trembling hand could barely strike the match. He took a glass of water for his throat which suddenly seemed dry and parched.

It was eight o'clock in the evening and he had been asleep for an hour.

Sam went downstairs, descending the spiral staircase past the elevator cage and into the main lobby. The wind had got up and the revolving doors were turning slowly. Through one of the windows Sam could see the trees in the street bending and twisting in the wind. Occasionally a drop of rain would rattle one of the window panes with a sound like a bullet. The staccato increased as the storm slowly folded itself around Sylow Springs.

He wanted to make a telephone call to Ellie. One of the phones still worked but he could not get through. In the end he hung up and went outside, standing for a while on the porch to let the strong wind clear his head and drive the nightmare from his mind. The rain was increasing in intensity and Sam ran to his car. He fumbled with the keys before clambering in. He sat in the car looking out over the deserted town as the rain started beating its hard metallic shell. He had the greatest urge to start up and simply go. If only he could be rid of this place once and for all. Why did his travels always end here?

He remained in the car for some time, feeling the strength of the storm surge around him. When it seemed to be subsiding he got out and went back into the hotel. All the lights were off now, only the clerk's desk seemed spared the deathly gloom that enveloped the building. Sitting beneath its circle of light the man continued ticking the newspaper columns. He did not look up as Sam crossed the lobby and returned to his room. As Sam slowly climbed the spiral staircase he saw to his surprise that the elevator had moved. It was no longer perched between two floors but had disappeared below the level of the lobby. When he reached his floor and turned off the staircase he suddenly heard the cables flap and as he looked down he saw the elevator coming up towards him. He watched as it rose past him and then stopped. Then, without any visible interference, it descended and came to a halt on his floor. Sam was startled by its unpredictable movements and slowly walked away.

Lightning continued to illuminate the corridors long after the rain and wind had died down. It was the only light, together with the neon sign. Back in his room Sam could consider himself lucky that he had at least this much extra light. But this provided scant comfort to him as the heavy lines of the old room recalled once more his nightmare. Now it seemed as if his room had been invaded by something hideous, venomous, malevolent. He doubted whether he could sleep again. Almost instinctively he crossed the room and pulled down the window and then, as an afterthought, locked the door. He lay on the bed and lit a cigarette. If he felt this strongly about it he could go back to Chicago by bus, he thought, but in the meantime he had to survive with the taste of death lingering in his mouth and the feeling of that other presence that now seemed a part of the room and of his world. Were they one and the same? Sam tried to shut the thought from his mind and with it the mouldering, crumbling room that seemed even now to be visibly decaying before his eyes. As a child, he had once fancied that the face of his mother on his portrait of her had moved. The illusion was a frightening one in a room shrouded and heavy. He recalled it now and with it the fear that it brought. Now it seemed as if this room too was taking on a life of its own—but not just a solitary portrait, the whole room!

It's always there Sam, the decay, the poverty. It's eating away all the time.

It was perhaps fortunate that Sam kept a bottle in his case. He needed it now and took several large glassfuls using the cup on the washstand. He was able to relax into the bed. The moving shifting room seemed more familiar now, the feeling of decay more mellow.

Sam slept poorly and when he awoke it was in fear of someone trying to get into his room. He was breathing heavily and the sound of his breath carried across the room and seemed to echo over the walls as if it were some tomb he had entered. He had dreamt of his wife, that she had appeared in front of him, drifting from the heavy drapes that enveloped the hallway. In the instant she had appeared she had been dragged back as if reclaimed. But the overwhelming fear was of some other presence and of a smell that only now he became aware of. It was the smell of decay—corruption! It was growing stronger. Could it be? Sam rose from the bed, it was becoming stronger still. It was as if the building was rotting, decomposing like a corpse laid to rest in the earth. He reached out with his arm and in the gloom he fancied that the wall crumbled to his touch. A fine dust seemed to stream down the wall and in horror he threw himself back. The smell grew stronger. Sam began choking, it made him weak and in panic he rushed to the door, fumbling with the lock in his scramble to be free of his room and the rotting building. Still the stench increased and as he pulled the door open at last, it seemed again as if the room were crumbling before his eyes.

Sam ran along the corridor, bringing his hand to his nose to cut out the stench that now made him gag and vomit. He dimly perceived the elevator. The door was open and he threw himself in, slamming the gate behind him. As he threw the switch and the elevator slowly descended, he caught a glimpse of his face in the mirror. A new wave of nausea devoured his senses for in the mirror he saw reflected not the corruption of elegant drapes and luxurious wallpaper but of flesh. Did his eyes deceive him or was it he who was decaying? His very face seemed to be decomposing and as he held up his hands, he saw in the dim light of the lobby that the flesh was slipping from the bone and crumbling to dust on the floor. He caught one more picture of his decay in the great splendid mirror of the hotel's main lobby—his body angled against the elegant brass bars of the cage. It hardly seemed to matter that the elevator did not stop on the ground floor as he had requested but continued its slow inexorable descent into the bowels of the old hotel.

Ken Dickson

THE SNORKEL, THE STARFISH AND THE SALT, SALT SEA

IN A GUST OF SUDDEN FEROCITY the wind drove needles into Robert Parker's face and scalp. Walking against the storm was like pushing against a body-building machine and he was exhausted when he turned, at last out of the full force of the gale, into the street where he lived.

Indoors, he leant back against the door as he closed it, feeling his cheeks tingle and the rain, dripping from his hair down inside his upturned collar, trickling in icy runnels down his back.

"That you already, Robert?" his wife Moira called from the kitchen.

"Who else? I'm not working late on my birthday, you know."

He threw his sodden raincoat over the back of a chair and moved towards the sitting-room. "God, it's a filthy night out there."

"Not yet!" Moira rushed past him into the sitting-room, thrusting a towel into his hands. "Dry yourself with that."

The door slammed in his face.

"You can't come in for a minute."

He heard her lifting things through the serving-hatch from the kitchen into the dining area and a moment later her voice. "Ready now."

He opened the door and Moira stood proudly by a table sparklingly set for two, patting a newly acquired hair-style into perfection with both hands. On the table stood bottles of champagne and claret alongside their best crystal glasses, and the first course, his favourite fried whitebait, was on the hot-plate.

Moira picked up a large, decoratively-wrapped parcel and held it out to him. "Happy birthday, darling."

"Well now, surprise, surprise," he smiled, moving forward to take it from her. "I didn't think you'd bother after all the rows we've had recently."

She really was an unpredictable woman, Robert thought as he set the surprisingly heavy parcel down on the floor and began carefully undoing the pink ribbon which enclosed it. He'd have thought a suit for divorce more likely than a birthday present. No especial reasons, just "incompatability". They were two people who simply could not live together without being constantly at each other's throats, and that was no way to live, even though they had agreed to go through with the holiday. Next day they were due to depart for a fortnight in Spain, booked many months before, in better times.

And now this.

"I know I've been awful at times, Robert, but you've been a bit of a swine yourself sometimes, you must admit. But I'd like to try again, if you will. I'm sure we can be happy together if we both really try. And the holiday is an ideal opportunity, isn't it?"

Robert looked up at her then from the parcel which he was still endeavouring to unwrap. Her long red hair was shining and provided a startling contrast to the new green dress. Obviously she had gone to considerable trouble (not to say expense, he winced inwardly) over this evening. But her emerald eyes, which normally either sparkled with laughter or flashed with anger, with no in-between stages, wore a pleading look he had never seen there before. He didn't like it, either.

"All right then, you're on," he laughed, and squeezed her hand. "But I'm dying to know what's in this."

Finally abandoning all attempt to remove the wrapping-paper intact, he ripped it off to reveal a large cardboard box containing a snorkel, face-mask, fins and other diving accoutrements. He remembered having mentioned to Moira on a previous visit to Spain that he would have liked to explore some of the small rocky coves and bays near the resort in which they stayed, and which had no beaches to attract the teeming throng, other than perhaps an occasional adventurous swimmer.

"That's marvellous," he said, putting his arms round her and kissing her on the forehead. "I shall enjoy using that. Thank you." He kissed her again, this time her mouth.

"I'm so glad." She pushed him away, but smiling now. "Come on, let's eat."

The dinner was a succession of his favourites. After the whitebait, a succulent steak and kidney pie with fresh vegetables, and fruit and Stilton to finish. They finished the wine and as Robert sat over brandy and coffee, Moira brought in a birthday cake she had baked that afternoon. It had one candle in the middle and "Happy Birthday Robert" piped around it, in pink icing.

"It's a few years since you made me one of those," he said, blowing out the candle.

"Did you wish?"

"Oh yes, I wished all right," he smiled, and cut two pieces of the cake.

When they had finished eating Robert rolled off his chair and lay on his back on the floor, his hands spread over his paunch. "I am replete," he stated.

He picked up the instruction booklet which had come with the snorkel and thumbed through it. "You know, you remind me of the sea," he said.

"You mean I'm deep and untameable, or I make you sick?"

"No," he laughed, "no old jokes now. I mean it. You've surprised me tonight. You can be so changeable, happy one day, completely impossible the next. Yet beneath it all you're still you. You never change really, all the different moods are just surface things. Like the sea," he finished a little self-consciously. They had not really spoken to each other for a long time, he realised. He held out his hand to her.

"Silly," she said, but took his hand and lay down beside him on the floor. She rested her head on his outstretched arm and looked closely into his eyes. She was still very beautiful, the green eyes such a complete opposite to that glorious shock of red hair, the finely flared nostrils, full red lips and firm chin. Indeed it would have been a perfect face, were it not for the inch-long, sickle-shaped scar in silver-white against the rose of one cheek, the result of a teenage riding accident.

They made love then, there on the carpet, and that was another thing they had not done for a long time. And afterwards they lay beside each other, playing records and drinking more brandy.

Moira chattered about the holiday, happy to feel relaxed after the months of tension between them, tension which had been both caused by their disintegrating relationship and then itself the cause of further disintegration. Robert did not say much.

They went to bed at a fairly early hour.

"We've got to be at the airport by 10.30," Moira was saying. "There's the 9.27 from Victoria which should get us there in nice time. That will mean getting a train from here around 8.30, so we'd better get a taxi about eight o'clock. What do you think?"

"I think that'll be just fine," Robert replied, amused at her excitement.

"There's not much to do in the morning. I've done most of the packing already so there's just a few last-minute things to throw into the suitcases. I *am* looking forward to the holiday now, Robert, are you?"

"Of course I am. Now come on, bed!" He took her elbow and steered her across the hall to their bedroom, pausing only to switch the lights off on the way.

In bed he leaned across and kissed her cheek before lying back beside her. "Thanks, Moira," he said, and felt her settle down in weary contentment.

He lay there long after she had gone to sleep, waiting.

The storm outside had long since abated and the night was still and silent.

About three o'clock Robert got carefully out of bed. He stepped quietly across the hall and into the bathroom, damning the creaking door. In a mirror he caught a glimpse of his pale face, framed by the black hair and beard. His dark eyes glinted oddly.

Opening a drawer, he pulled forth a long, black object from which, as he lifted it, the blade swung open, gleaming in a sudden shaft of moonlight.

On eggshell tread, he stepped back into the darkened bedroom.

Moira, still soundly asleep, snored softly.

In a moment Robert had moved, he had glided to her side and clamped thumb and forefinger, firmly, over her nose.

The snoring stopped, to be replaced by her spluttering cough as she awoke. Her uncomprehending eyes looked up into his wild ones, and then her bewilderment turned to horror as the razor arced down.

So sharp was the blade that she felt no pain, but only an instant of coldness on her throat and then her own hot blood flooding the pillow. Then she was dead.

Only then did Robert consider what to do next. He was tempted to leave her there till he came back from holiday, all her friends would assume she was on holiday with him, of course. But then the thought of decay, with the possibility that the smell might arouse the suspicion of a postman or someone, occurred to him.

So he climbed up into the loft, emptied the contents out of an old tea-chest and lowered that down.

He wrapped Moira in her bloody sheets and stuffed her body, pillow, razor and all into the chest and shut it tight. Then he dragged it out to the garden shed, being careful to keep to the concrete path so as to leave no marks on the grass, and locked it in.

Fortunately the bungalow stood in a fairly large garden all round so there was no possibility it would be noticed there.

"That'll do nicely till I get back," Robert thought, going back indoors. "Then I can drive it somewhere one night and dump it."

He would have to leave the house eventually, of course, but there was no hurry. It would be many weeks, or even months, after he got back before Moira's friends and neighbours (she had no close relatives) grew suspicious enough to do anything if he told them she had been taken ill in Spain and detained in hospital.

Certainly there was no sense in spoiling a good holiday over it.

Robert decided not to wait in case the neighbours noticed him leaving alone, so he phoned for a taxi immediately.

By seven-thirty he was sitting in the cafeteria at Gatwick airport, drinking coffee and eating scrambled eggs on toast.

When he checked in his luggage, one small brown suitcase and a holdall containing the new diving gear, he explained to the girl that he was travelling alone because his wife had recently left him. Really she was quite sympathetic.

Then he strolled around the busy concourse until the time for his flight, amused at the obvious Spanish-holiday "arrivals", the tanned women in sombreros and children struggling to carry enormous stuffed donkeys.

Soon he heard his flight called and joined the queue for boarding.

He sat by the window with the spare seat on his right. The outside seat of the rank of three was taken by a short, attractive, dyed-blonde woman who had been separated from her son on the other side of the gangway by the lottery of seat allocations. She leaned across to Robert.

"Excuse me, do you know if this seat will be occupied?"

"Er, no, it won't. My wife won't be travelling."

"Then would it be all right if Terry sat here? We're on our own and he is a little bit nervous. First flight, you know? So am I for that matter," she giggled.

Robert had assumed the boy was also with the people on the other side of him and had rather looked forward to having a spare seat beside him—these package flights were cramped enough—but could hardly refuse. So Terry was installed on his right and, in fact, did not seem in the least nervous, though his mother certainly was.

A thin, bespectacled lad about ten years old, he started chatting to Robert immediately, asking him more questions about the plane than Robert was able to answer, and his sharp elbow dug into Robert's thigh as he leaned across to look out when the plane taxied on to the runway for take-off. As soon as they were permitted to unfasten their seat-belts, Robert offered to exchange seats with the boy, if only to stop the rather painful pressure on his thigh.

And, as a result, was unable to avoid being drawn into conversation with Terry's mother. Maureen, her name was, as he soon found out. Indeed, over the next two hours there was little he did *not* find out about her. A widow for some three years, times had been hard and when a small legacy came her way she decided to spend it on a "proper" holiday for herself and the boy, something they had not been able to afford since her husband died.

On arrival at Gerona, they found themselves boarding the same coach for their destination, bound for different but practically adjacent hotels.

Robert rather liked the slim, vivacious woman and thought her cheerful talkativeness might make her an agreeable holiday companion. She was the complete opposite of Moira, whose see-sawing moods of black, aggressive despondency and near-hysterical happiness he finally could endure no longer. He took to the boy as well, whose serious but interested personality reminded him of his own youth, or even of the son his late, unlamented wife had been unable to give him.

So, after booking in to his hotel, leaving his luggage on the bed of a room all but identical to thousands of others on the Costa Brava, small, clean and adequate, and quickly eating the hotel's buffet-style lunch, Robert walked out in the hot June sunshine to meet Maureen and Terry.

Being a regular visitor to the resort he had happily volunteered to show the couple around. Indeed, he had momentarily entertained the idea of continuing the relationship when the holiday was over (he sensed Maureen would like to) but quickly realised the impossibility of doing so. When the police investigated his wife's disappearance, as eventually they must, those on his flight and in his hotel would inevitably be questioned. No, he would have to "disappear" completely, and sever all ties with his home and this holiday.

But that was a long way in the future. For the moment he was determined to enjoy the next fortnight to the full.

Maureen and Terry were waiting for him when he turned the corner to their hotel, and together they walked down towards the beach, only a hundred yards or so distant. As they walked, Maureen put her arm in his, already assuming, in her relaxed manner, a familiarity which Robert was happy to accept.

"I thought we'd just walk around this afternoon, if that's all right with you? Let you get to know the place a bit," Robert explained.

"You're the guide. Lead on, MacDuff," Maureen smiled, cuddling his arm closer.

Robert felt the tension and anxiety sloughing off him already like dead skin as they walked.

He always felt at ease in Spain, right from the first moment at the airport when that unmistakeable odour, compounded of tobacco, sunshine and who knows what else, hit his nostrils.

They stood for a while surveying the beach, the wide, white

expanse of hot shingle nearly empty as always, except for a row of humanity about four people deep, which stretched along the edge of the sea from one end of the beach to the other, in a colourful riot of parasols, deck-chairs and wind-breaks.

"Is that a castle, Robert?" Terry asked, indicating the little white crenellated tower and wall which capped the rocky promontory to their left.

And Robert explained, in a happily quasi-paternal manner, the little he knew of the building and also of the bronze statue of the fisher-maid which stood atop the low cliffs at the other end of the beach.

The chance male and female characters of the structures at either end of the beach struck Robert then, as never before. The very male battlemented building to their left guarding the land from the sea's encroachments while the fisher-girl, arm welcomingly upraised, besought its bounty as one female to another.

Then they walked on along the front towards the little castle, Robert and Maureen arm in arm, each slightly exhilarated at the realisation that they had found a partner for the holiday. Terry strolled gravely by his mother's side, though once he ran off to peer into the window of a seafood restaurant where, in a tank of seawater, brown crayfish clambered over their companions as if they were rocks.

The ascending path to the castle, which proved when they got there not to be one at all (though there was no admission to the tower), became a short tunnel cut through the solid rock of the promontory itself, ending in a little viewing platform from which the unscaleable cliff-face descended to the blue peacefulness of a tiny cove.

"Doesn't that water look inviting down there?" Robert said. "I've got a new snorkel diving outfit I brought to explore some of the little bays like that just along the coast. Although I must admit I don't even know how to use it properly yet."

"Have you really, Robert?" Terry asked with unexpected

enthusiasm. "Can I help you with it?"

"He's in the sub-aqua club at school," Maureen explained. "He knows all about it, though of course he's not old enough to have a full diving kit of his own yet."

"That's great. You can explain it to me then," Robert laughed. "Tell you what, tomorrow morning we'll go for a swim, right?"

"Yes please! Look, what's that, Mum?" Terry asked then, pouncing to pick something up from the rocks at their feet. It was the brown, hard skeleton of a starfish. Robert took it, staring at it in some surprise. In its centre was a disturbingly familiar, nacreous mark, shaped like a sickle. Robert thought at first it had been scratched on to the brown surface, but closer inspection revealed that it was in fact an inherent part of the object.

He lost his temper then and hurled the starfish out over the edge, watching it spin in a slow cartwheel all the way down to where it entered, in a tiny splash of white, the blue water far below.

The look of disappointment on Terry's face made Robert feel ashamed of his loss of self-control over what was obviously no more than an extraordinary coincidence, and he took mother and son by their respective elbows, guiding them back down towards the beach, saying "Come on, I'll buy us all a drink."

They sat outside a cafe for a while, absorbing the heat, Terry with a coke, his mother with a coffee. ("Café con leche, you must ask for," Robert explained to her.) Robert had a beer.

Then they strolled around the centre of the town itself, Maureen keeping up a constant stream of happy, meaningless chatter and insisting on entering every tourist gift-shop they came to, and there were hundreds of them. She tried on straw hats and examined ornamental shells and model matadors with joyful fascination, and was so dizzily incapable of calculating the sterling equivalent of the prices of things with any accuracy that once, after a particularly wild guess at the true cost of a leather handbag, Robert was so amused that he could not resist kissing her.

Maureen's blue eyes looked seriously into his dark ones for a moment, and she squeezed his hand, then the laughter returned and they were off to look into yet another shop selling identical goods.

Later, she invited Robert back to her hotel for a drink of the duty-free Scotch she had bought on the plane and while Terry, in goggles and flippers, splashed about in the swimming pool downstairs, they made love on her creaky, narrow bed.

When it was over, Robert held her hot, naked body close to him, breathing in the salt smell of her, until they heard Terry banging on the door of the little room. Then he dressed and went back to his own hotel.

He showered and changed and took the lift down to the hotel restaurant where he was placed at a table with a young honeymoon couple from Birmingham. They had been there a week already, the girl nicely tanned, the boy's face the colour of tinned salmon, and told Robert to expect very little of the food. In the event it turned out to be quite edible, though as an attempt at making an English meal from Spanish ingredients, and cooked in a Spanish manner, it fell rather limply between the two stools. Robert had always felt that these hotels would do best to stick to Spanish cooking, but a glance at the packets of cornflakes, pots of jam etc. which decorated many of the tables, suggested that most of the hotel's gastronomically unadventurous English clientele would not.

After dinner Robert ambled over to the other hotel and sat with a beer in the bar, waiting for Maureen and Terry to come down. When they did, he saw that she had changed into a blue dress with a white shawl. Terry still wore the same tee-shirt, jeans and sneakers, and his solemn face broke into a rare smile behind the thick, round spectacles when he recognised Robert.

Robert tousled the boy's short, sandy hair and led them out into the still warm evening.

"Tonight being Saturday there's a dance for the locals in the town square, that's at one end of the gardens on the sea-front. It's well worth seeing, the band is really good, very unusual, and the dance is a sort of Catalonian speciality, called Sardanes a la Plaça. I believe it starts about ten, so we have time for a stroll and a drink before then, if you'd like?"

They were happy to have their evening arranged for them (Robert felt they would have fallen in with anything he suggested) and accordingly, they made their way back down to the sea-front. While they were sitting on the wall along the edge of the beach, watching the sun set over the mountains above and behind the town, the young couple whose table Robert shared walked past, obviously surprised and a little embarrassed to see him hand in hand with Maureen. They said hello, but giggled as they walked on, whispering to each other.

Later, seated on small barrels in a bodega which Robert knew from previous visits, Maureen scrutinised the range of liqueurs in barrels which occupied the whole of one wall, and vowed to try them all before the holiday was over.

"I'll try the apricot brandy first. No I won't, the crème de cacao. No, wait, what's 'huevos'?"

"Eggs, I think," Robert laughed.

"Yeuk! No, 'anis', that's aniseed, isn't it? That'll do."

Terry had another coke, with a small saucerful of mussels, and Robert a coñac. For all his quiet seriousness, Robert could sense that the boy was happy to be with them, and proud to be accepted without question in such a 'grown-up' place.

The conversation was amusing and relaxed, though once, after the first couple of drinks, Maureen asked a question which brought Robert up sharp.

"What did you say happened to your wife?"

"I don't believe I did say," he replied, licking his lower lip. "But she died. About, er, three months ago. The holiday was already booked so I decided to come alone. It's been a bad time and I really needed to get away."

"Oh, I see." Maureen's freckled face crinkled into a sympathetic, yet somehow enigmatic smile, and Robert felt, for the first time, that unsuspected depths underlay the woman's cheerful and straightforward surface.

Over the next hour or so, however, Maureen made a confident start towards achieving her target and Robert happily kept pace with her, drinking beer and coñac. Then, just after ten o'clock, the sound of the band tuning up drifted into the crowded bodega. Robert paid the bill, giving the barman a few pesetas tip, which provoked a ringing of bells behind the bar. Then, in the gathering night, they strolled back down the narrow alleyway to the square.

The band, which they viewed against a backdrop of palm-trees, hibiscus and the dark sea itself, was basically a brass one with, for contrast, a couple of unusual woodwind instruments, the predominant one of which produced a curious braying tone rather like an overblown soprano saxophone. A double bass provided the rhythmic pulse, a repeated figure in which the first three beats were accented evenly. The townspeople danced in a wide circle, holding hands and performing the slow and dignified steps while the circle revolved. Before tourism came to dominate the area they had been fisherfolk, and the dance was a relic of that era, a celebration of the bounty and (temporary) mercy of their great, wilful mother, the sea.

Terry, especially, was enchanted with the sight of the dancers and the sound of the music in the warm, scented Mediterranean night and refused to return to bed until the entertainment was finally over.

When it was, Robert walked them back to their hotel, Maureen clutching his left hand and Terry his right. Tired and content, even Maureen was no longer talkative. Robert kissed her goodnight and confirmed with Terry their arrangements to go swimming the following morning.

But when they had gone, he did not feel like retiring immediately. Enjoyable as the day had been, there was something which flawed his contentment and nagged at his brain.

He sat in a quiet bar and drank a couple more coñacs before giving up and returning to his hotel. But he could not sleep. The night was warm and unusually humid for Spain, and Robert lay naked and sweating on top of the bed covers. He could not forget that starfish. How had it got to the top of the cliff, for one thing? Well, obviously someone had found it on the beach and carried it up there. There was no other explanation, he told himself. And the sickle-shaped mark? Coincidence, that was all. That species probably all bore identical marks.

But it was a long time before he slept.

The morning was already hot and sunny when Robert awoke and pulled aside the thick curtains. He shaved, showered and dressed in fifteen minutes and only just made it to the dining-room before the breakfast sitting was over. His young table-mates had already eaten and gone, to judge by the debris on his table, and he was glad to eat his rolls and coffee alone.

Then he collected the bag containing the diving equipment from his room and went out to meet Maureen and Terry. The heat struck him like a weight the instant he stepped outside the hotel.

They were waiting at the bus-stop when he got there, and Robert gave them each a kiss, to the boy's obvious embarrassment.

"Morning each," he pronounced, "all ready to go swimming then?"

"Terry is, but I'm not," Maureen declared. "My bathing costume is strictly for *sun*-bathing, not sea-bathing!"

"There's no beach where we're going, you know. Still, I expect we can find you a nice flat rock to stretch out on, unless you'd like to stay here and Terry and I will go on our own?"

"Oh no," she laughed ruefully, "I'm coming to keep my eye on you two!"

The little, single-decker bus rolled up then and Robert paid the few pesetas fare, which took them to the terminus at Canyelles, some three miles up the coast. For most of the journey they could see the Mediterranean, calm and silver-blue, far down on their right-hand side. To the left, from time to time, they caught a glimpse of mountain tops through the pines, shimmering in the heat.

Disembarking, they did not follow the other few passengers to the small, sandy beach but walked on, following the same dusty road for another quarter of a mile before cutting through the fragrant pines on a steeply descending footpath to the sea.

At length they emerged on to the rock-strewn shore of a little bay, deserted save for a small party of Germans on the rocky point to their right.

"Here we are," Robert exclaimed. "Nice and quiet, isn't it?" He led the way to the left.

Maureen smiled doubtfully, and took his hand to steady herself as they stepped tentatively over the uneven surface.

"This should do, I think." Robert stopped when he came to a flat rock just large enough for Maureen to lie down. "What do you think?"

Maureen looked around. The voices of the Germans across the water and the sound of the gentle waves splashing on to the shore were all that disturbed the silence. Unaccountably, she shivered.

"A bit too quiet for me, I'm afraid. Still, you boys go on and enjoy yourselves."

She took a large, green towel out of the bag she carried, spread it out and sat down, taking off her beach-robe to reveal the bikini which was all she wore underneath.

Robert winked approval. "Now come on, Terry, you were going to explain how this thing works to me."

He lifted the diving gear out of his bag. There was a booklet of directions for use but disdaining this, Terry had soon conveyed the basic principles to him and confidently led him forth to the water's edge.

"Don't you go too far out now, Terry," Maureen enjoined.

"I won't!" he yelled back.

They sat on the rocks and donned their flippers, and Terry helped Robert to get his snorkel and face-mask in order. Terry himself had one of those plastic gadgets containing a ping-pong ball and soon was splashing delightedly back and forth, first in a large and surprisingly deep rock-pool, then in the sea itself.

It took Robert some time to master the breathing, and several mouthfuls of the very salt water before he finally submerged with a clear face-plate, despite Terry's expert advice. But when he did it was to a new world.

The sea, cold at first to his hot skin, was in fact amniotically warm and so buoyant that Robert, not an especially strong swimmer, was soon propelling himself easily along with the fins, way out past Terry, lost in childlike fascination at the profusion of marine life around him.

The sea-bed was basically sandy, though here and there rocky outgrowths broke through, some to considerable heights.

Small, brightly-coloured fish, and even some surprisingly large ones, darted to and fro, and in the heavy, weedy undergrowth Robert caught signs of movement which he didn't have the nerve to investigate.

He surfaced, expelling water from his tube before breathing as Terry had taught him, and swam back to the boy who sat toying with something by the water's edge.

"Look Robert, it's the same one we found yesterday."

Terry handed him the faded, brown skeleton of a starfish. It had a white sickle-shape in the centre.

Disconcerted, Robert stared at it for a moment.

"Nonsense. It's probably just a species common to these parts."

Maureen came over to see what they had found and peered over his shoulder. "It looks like the same one, Robert," she said, "look, one of the points is slightly broken underneath in just the same way. I wonder how it got all the way along here."

Glancing at her, Robert once more had the feeling that beneath her placid surface was a mystery, a wealth perhaps of purely feminine lore which would be for ever hidden from him. Like the sea, he thought, remembering some of his last words to his wife.

"Strange, isn't it?" Maureen continued. "I don't think I like this place much, you know. From now on I shall stick to the main beach."

"Don't be silly," Robert said, forcing a smile. "I suppose it's possible the current carried it this far, but much more likely it's just a similar one which also happens to be broken."

Rather guiltily, he tossed it back in the water. "Come on, Terry, let's swim."

Robert stayed close to the bottom then, keeping the steep rock wall of the point on his left. The water was glassy clear and it wasn't till he looked for the surface that he realised how deep he was, and how steeply the sea-floor shelved away from the shore.

Surprised and a little perturbed, he turned and swam back.

Terry was sitting by his mother when he got there, and helped Robert unfasten the apparatus.

"You should try it, Maureen, it's fantastically warm and clear." He leaned over and kissed the drop of briny sweat off her nose.

"Not likely, I'm strictly a landlubber," she smiled, but it seemed to Robert that her eyes, behind the sunglasses, looked not at him but rather anxiously out to sea, as if puzzled.

Robert stood till the sun had dried him off somewhat, then smothered himself with sun-tan oil and sat down.

From the depths of her bag Maureen produced three enormous salami-filled rolls and handed them out, then a large bottle of fizzy orange drink.

"Saves rushing back to the hotel for lunch, doesn't it?"

Robert kissed her again. Her hot skin smelled of sweat and sun-tan lotion. "Good idea."

After he had eaten, Robert stood up and looked around the cove. Across the water the Germans were still the only other people in sight. The three men were diving off the end of the point into the deep water while their wives or girl-friends lay, face-down, improving their already well established tans.

"Well, I'm going in again, anybody coming?" Robert asked.

"No, I think I'll look for crabs for a bit," Terry said, while Maureen merely smiled her refusal.

This time Robert swam on the sparkling surface of the water out to the centre of the bay, then dove straight down and followed the bottom back to the middle of the little headland, which was about as far as he had got earlier. Again he was astonished at the numbers and variety of the fish which swam round him, making little effort to avoid him. Indeed, he frequently felt their small, hard bodies brush his chest and legs.

After surfacing and refilling his lungs, Robert decided to follow the wall of the headland out to its end, it shouldn't be beyond his limit, to see what lay round the other side. Occasionally he saw a flurry of sand on the bottom as some small creature scuttled from one clump of weeds to another.

The water grew colder and steadily more opaque as he swam out and the depth increased, but still Robert could see a considerable distance. He kept close to the steep incline on his left.

Then he saw looming towards him, from straight ahead, what he at first took to be an unusually large white fish. It was difficult to be certain of size and distance, but nevertheless he felt panic rising within him. Were there sharks in the Med.? He thought there were porbeagles, and possibly baskers also. Harmless things anyway.

But whatever this was, though obviously still some way off, it seemed to be coming straight at him in an extremely aggressive and businesslike manner. Robert saw that from round its head trailed red fins, or some kind of strange growth, seaweed possibly, of a carmine hue.

He turned then, treading water fast, trying to propel himself towards the surface which looked unbelievably high above him. The oncoming form changed direction to intercept him.

As it swam quickly closer, Robert saw that what he had taken for red fins did not, in fact, look like fins at all. Really, it looked more like long red hair.

Maureen was lying face-down, bra-strap undone, drowsily soaking in the hot sunshine when she felt the warm hand on her back. It was her son.

"What is it, Terry?" she asked, sitting up and fastening the bikini-top.

"It's Robert, Mum. He's been gone an awfully long time."

Maureen pulled her watch out of the bag and was amazed to see how late it was. She had slept longer than she realised.

"Haven't you seen him come to the surface recently?" she asked the boy.

"I haven't noticed him, though he could have surfaced out of sight somewhere. But he's not a very experienced diver. He should have come back by now."

"Well, don't worry. He's probably sitting on the beach round in the next bay," Maureen said, trying to sound more confident than she felt. There was something wrong about this place, she had felt it from the first. "Woman's intuition" maybe.

But as time wore on they grew more and more anxious, and eventually decided to walk out along the little headland, treading gingerly on the sometimes viciously sharp rocks, to see if they could spot Robert in the clear water beneath. It wasn't until they were almost at the end of the point that they saw the white form bobbing to and fro against the rocks, with the lapping waves.

Hearing Maureen's scream, the three Germans swam across the bay and had reached the spot before Maureen and Terry had clambered down to the water's edge.

Together, they dragged Robert's body out of the water and

laid it on the rocks.

There were several grazes and contusions on his chest and arms and legs, doubtless caused by the repeated contact with the rocks. But it was difficult to believe that any rock, or for that matter anything other than a razor, could be quite so sharp as to slice open Robert's throat, from ear to ear, quite so comprehensively.

Maureen put her hand on her son's shoulder, tasting the salt sweat on her top lip, as she gazed out across the vast blue deep.

Elizabeth Fancett

A STRANGE AND AWFUL COINCIDENCE

THE CAVE WAS VERY DARK. AND it was narrow. He could touch both walls at the same time.

Where was he? And how had he got here? He'd obviously fallen—but from where? He reckoned he must have been stunned by his fall, for he could remember nothing.

Feeling bruised and still dazed, he scrambled to his feet. Something bumped against his side. Some sort of haversack? He fumbled with the fastening. Perhaps it contained a torch, or some matches? But his groping fingers touched only a soft package—probably sandwiches—another package which felt like biscuits, two apples and a banana.

So he'd brought food with him! Surely that should tell him something? He tried hard to remember, but his mind persisted in blankness. He looked up, scanning the dark ceiling. Not even a chink of light showed.

All right . . . think this out! Calmly, rationally. *That* was a good start, he reflected. At least he knew he must be a person who could view a situation—however drastic—calmly, or he wouldn't have been able to decide to do just that, would he?

Now, if the opening through which he'd fallen wasn't directly overhead then he must have wandered this far away from it. Then, still dazed by his fall, he'd probably collapsed and passed out again.

He frowned. No. He wasn't given to passing out, not even under extreme circumstances. Or *was* he? He didn't know, did he? He didn't know *anything*—not who he was, or where he was, or how he came to be here.

Think now, think! He'd brought food . . . what could that tell him? Perhaps he'd been on a hike somewhere . . . a heath, a moor . . . somewhere where there were caves? He'd been on holiday perhaps . . .?

The blankness of his mind began to frighten him. No, *that* wouldn't do! If there was anything he despised, it was fear. At least he knew that much about himself, didn't he? He was the non-panicking sort. He *must* be, or he wouldn't be trying to rationalise like this.

Now, he'd fallen into this cave and wandered away from the opening. But which way had he come? He didn't want to waste precious time by moving away from it. Still, he had to make a start somewhere. He might be lucky enough to get it right first time. If not, he'd just have to go on until he came to a dead end. Then he'd come back again and keep on in the other direction.

With a hand on each of the walls he edged along in the darkness. The cave seemed endless. The walls remained smooth and unbroken in surface and no trace of light showed from above.

He stopped. Surely he couldn't have come *this* far from the opening? How long had he been going now . . . ten . . . twenty minutes? It seemed like hours. Perhaps he should have gone the other way after all.

He started to turn back when his hand touched another hand—cold, clammy fingers against one of the walls. He drew away sharply, stifling a scream. If there was one thing he couldn't stand it was a man screaming. The owner of the hand he had touched had no such aversion.

"That's enough!" he said sharply. "I'm in the same position as you are!"

"But how did we *get* here?" came a voice from the darkness.

"We fell!" he said irritably. Another thing he couldn't stand was daft questions. "How long have you been coming in this direction?"

"Who knows!" The voice was near to hysteria. "Ten . . . twenty minutes. It seems like hours!"

"Can you remember anything . . . before you fell?"

"Not a thing. I just—found myself here."

"Well," he said, "it seems we've both been moving away from our point of entry."

Point of entry! *That* was a euphemism in the circumstances! He grinned in the darkness—which was a good thing, he thought. He must obviously have a sense of humour, which would stand him in good stead. Stand them both in good stead, he reflected wryly, judging by the exactly opposite nature of his fellow unfortunate.

"Well," he said cheerfully, "let's each continue the way we're going. We both might have missed something. If we find anything . . . a chink of light . . . a draught of air . . . we'll shout."

"No!" said the other voice harshly. "Let's stay together!"

"Get going!" he said gruffly. He hated and despised fear. He was sure of that, at least. Without waiting for an answer, he shuffled past his unseen companion and moved on again, his feet making no sound on the soft earthy floor.

The silence continued for a long time. He reckoned by now they must have travelled some distance from each other—that was if the other fellow hadn't given up and was sitting down somewhere. No point in calling out to him. He'd probably jump out of his skin with fright—that is if he could hear him!

He stopped. It was no use, he'd have to go back. The opening he'd fallen through must be in the other direction. God knows from which point the other fellow had fallen in.

He was turning round when his hand touched another hand against the wall. A familiar scream split the silence.

"It's only me, you fool!" he said, angry with shock. "We must be in a circular cave! We've been moving towards each other."

"Then we're trapped!" The voice was hysterical and edged with screams.

"Nonsense!" he rasped. "We fell in—so there *must* be a way out! Anyway, someone's bound to miss us. All we have to do is sit tight. Do you happen to have any food with you?"

"F—food?"

"Yes, you know—the stuff you eat!"

"I've some in my haversack."

"How much?"

"Some sandwiches and biscuits . . . two apples I think . . . oh, and a banana."

So have I! he thought. *Exactly* the same! And he felt somehow that that mattered. It certainly was a strange coincidence. Maybe they'd both come from some inn or pub and the manager had put them up a standard packed lunch?

"Well," he said, "that should last us until we're rescued. Let's eat!"

But he heard only himself rustling in the darkness as he groped in his haversack for the sandwiches.

"No good starving!" he grunted. "Here—have one of mine!"

To his horror he heard the sound of weeping.

"Stop it!" he shouted. "If there's anything I can't stand, it's a man crying! Stop it! Or I'll make you stop it!"

The weeping turned to screaming. Reaching in the darkness, he felt and seized a head, started to bang it against the wall of the cave. He banged and smashed and went on smashing long after the screams had stopped.

They found him a few days later. By the light of a powerful torch they saw him slumped against the dark wall, his head a battered bloody mess, a half-eaten sandwich mouldering in the dirt and blood and slime of the cave floor.

"Poor devil!" said the administrator of the home. "He was always running away. But how did you know where to look?"

"Someone heard screams," said the constable. "The caves and potholes are notorious on these moors, and there are several covered by thick undergrowth. One could fall in anywhere in a dozen different places and never find a way out again. Was he a bad case?"

"Very bad," said the administrator. "He was a severe schizophrenic."

Brian Lumley

SNARKER'S SON

"ALL RIGHT, ALL RIGHT!" SERGEANT SCOTT noisily submitted. "So you're lost. You're staying with your dad here in the city at a hotel—you went sightseeing and you got separated—I accept all that. But look, son, we've had lost kids in here before, often, and they didn't try on all this silly stuff about names and spellings and all!"

Sergeant Scott had known—had been instinctively "aware" all day—that this was going to be one of *those* shifts. Right up until ten minutes ago his intuition had seemed for once to have let him down. But now . . .

"It's true," the pallid, red-eyed nine-year-old insisted, hysteria in his voice. "It's all true, everything I've said. This town *looks* like Mondon—but it's not! And . . . and before I came in here I passed a store called Woolworths—but it should have been 'Wolwords!'"

"All right, let's not start that again," the policeman put up quieting hands. "Now: you say you came down with your father from . . . from Sunderpool? That's in England?"

"No, I've *told* you," the kid started to cry again. "It's 'Eenland!' We came down on holiday from Sunderpool by longcar, and——"

"Longcar?" Sergeant Scott cut in, frowning. "Is that some place on the north-east coast?"

"No, it's not a place! A longcar is . . . well, a *longcar*! Like a buzz but longer, and it goes on the longcar lanes. You know . . .?" The boy looked as puzzled as Sergeant Scott, to say nothing of accusing.

"No, I don't know!" the policeman shook his head, trying to control his frown. "A 'buzz?'" Scott could feel the first twinges of one of his bilious headaches coming on, and so decided to change the subject.

"What does your father do, son? He's a science-fiction writer, eh?—And you're next in a long line?"

"Dad's a snarker," the answer came quite spontaneously, without any visible attempt at deceit or even flippancy. In any case, the boy was obviously far too worried to be flippant. A "nut", Scott decided—but nevertheless a nut in trouble.

Now the kid had an inquisitive look on his face. "What's science-fiction?" he asked.

"Science fiction," the big sergeant answered with feeling, "is that part of a policeman's lot called 'desk-duty'—when crazy lost kids walk into the station in tears to mess up said policeman's life!"

His answer set the youngster off worse than before.

Sighing, Scott passed his handkerchief across the desk and stood up. He called out to a constable in an adjacent room:

"Hey, Bob, come and look after the desk until Sergeant Healey gets in, will you? He's due on duty in the next ten minutes or so. I'll take the kid and see if I can find his father. If I can't—well, I'll bring the boy back here and the job can go through the usual channels."

"All right, sergeant, I'll watch the shop," the constable agreed as he came into the duty-room and took his place at the desk. "I've been listening to your conversation! Right rum 'un that," he grinned, nodding towards the tearful boy. "What an imagination!"

Imagination, yes. And yet Scott was not quite sure. There was "something in the air", a feeling of impending—*strangeness*—hard to define.

"Come on, son," he said, shaking off his mood. "Let's go."

He took the boy's hand. "Let's see if we can find your dad. He's probably rushing about right now wondering what's become of you." He shook his head in feigned defeat and said: "I don't know—ten o'clock at night, just going off duty—and *you* have to walk in on me!"

"Ten o'clock—*already*?" The boy looked up into Scott's face with eyes wider and more frightened than ever. "Then we only have half an hour!"

"Eh?" the policeman frowned again as they passed out into the London street (or was it "Mondon", Scott wondered with a mental grin). "Half an hour? What happens at half past ten, son? Do you turn into a pumpkin or something?" His humour was lost on his small charge.

"I mean the *lights*!" the boy answered, in what Scott took to be exasperation. "That's when the lights go out. At half past ten they put the lights out."

"They do?" the sergeant had given up trying to penetrate the boy's fertile but decidedly warped imagination. "Why's that, I wonder?" (Let the kid ramble on; it was better than tears at any rate.)

"Don't you know *anything*?" the youngster seemed half-astonished, half-unbelieving, almost as if he thought Scott was pulling his leg.

"No," the sergeant returned, "I'm just a stupid copper! But come on—where did you give your father the slip? You said you passed Woolworths getting to the police station. Well, Woolworths is down this way, near the tube." He looked at the boy sharply in mistaken understanding. "You didn't get lost on the tube, did you? Lots of kids do when it's busy."

"The Tube?" Scott sensed that the youngster spoke the words in capitals—and yet it was only a whisper. He had to hold on tight as the boy strained away from him in something akin to horror. "No one goes down in The Tube any more, except——" He shuddered.

"Yes?" Scott pressed, interested in this particular part of the boy's fantasy despite himself and the need, now, to have done with what would normally be a routine job. "Except who?"

"Not *who*," the boy told him, clutching his hand tighter. "Not who, but——"

"But?" again, patiently, Scott prompted him.

"Not who but *what*!"

"Well, go on," said the sergeant, sighing, leading the way down the quiet, half-deserted street towards Woolworths. "*What*, er, goes down in the tube?"

"Why, Tubers, of course!" Again there was astonishment in the youngster's voice, amazement at Scott's obvious deficiency in general knowledge. "Aren't you Mondoners thick!" It was a statement of fact, not a question.

"Right," said Scott, not bothering to pursue the matter further, seeing the pointlessness of questioning an idiot. "We've passed Woolworths—now where?"

"Over there, I think, down that street. Yes!—that's where I lost my father—down there!"

"Come on," Scott said, leading the boy across the road, empty now of all but the occasional car, down into the entrance of the indicated street. In fact it was little more than an alley, dirty and unlighted. "What on earth were you doing down here in the first place?"

"We weren't down here," the youngster answered with a logic that made the sergeant's head spin. "We were in a bright street, with lots of lights. Then I felt a funny buzzing feeling, and . . . and then I was here! I got frightened and ran."

At that moment, their footsteps echoing hollowly on the cobbles of the alley, the sergeant felt a weird vibration that began in his feet and travelled up his body to his head, causing a burst of bright, painfully bilious stars to flash across his vision—and simultaneous with this peculiar sensation the two turned a corner to emerge with startling abruptness into a much brighter side street.

"That was the buzzing I told you about," the boy stated unnecessarily.

Scott was not listening. He was looking behind him for the

broken electric cable he felt sure must be lying there just inside the alley (the sensation must surely have been caused by a mild electric shock), but he couldn't see one. Nor could he see anything else that might have explained that tingling, nerve-rasping sensation he had known. For that matter, where was the entrance (or exit) from which he and the boy had just this second emerged?

Where was the alley?

"Dad!" the kid yelled, suddenly tugging himself free to go racing off down the street.

Scott stood and watched, his head starting to throb and the street lights flaring garishly before his eyes. At the boy's cry a lone man had turned, started to run, and now Scott saw him sweep the lad up in his arms and wildly hug him, intense and obvious relief showing in his face.

The policeman forgot the problem of the vanishing alley and walked up to them, hands behind his back in the approved fashion, smiling benignly. "Cute lad you've got there, sir—but I should curb his imagination if I were you. Why, he's been telling me a story fit to——"

Then the benign smile slid from his face. "*Here!*" he cried, his jaw dropping in astonishment.

But despite his exclamation, Scott was nevertheless left standing on his own. For without a word of thanks both man and boy had made off down the street, hands linked, running as if the devil himself was after them!

"Here!" the policeman called again, louder. "Hold on a bit——"

For a moment the pair stopped and turned, then the man glanced at his watch (reminding Scott curiously of the White Rabbit in *Alice in Wonderland*) before picking up the boy again and holding him close. "Get off the street!" he yelled back at Scott as he once more started to run. "Get off the streets, man." His white face glanced back and up at the street lights as he ran, and Scott saw absolute fear shining in his eyes. "It'll soon be half past ten!"

The policeman was still in the same position, his jaw hanging slack, some seconds later when the figure of the unknown man, again hugging the boy to him, vanished round a distant corner. Then he shrugged his shoulders and tried to pull himself together, setting his helmet more firmly on his aching head.

"Well I'll be——" he grinned nervously through the throb of his headache. "Snarker's son, indeed!"

Alone, now, Scott's feeling of impending—*something*—returned, and he noticed suddenlv just how deserted the street was. He had never known London so quiet before. Why, there wasn't a single soul in sight!

And a funny thing, but here he was, only a stone's throw from his station, where he'd worked for the last fifteen years of his life, and yet—damned if he could recognise the street! Well, he knew he'd brought the boy down a dark, cobbled alley from the right, and so . . .

He took the first street on the right, walking quickly down it until he hit another street he knew somewhat better——

—Or did he?

Yes, yes, of course he did. The street was deserted now, quite empty, but just over there was good old . . .

Good old Wolwords!

Lights blazed and burst into multicoloured sparks before Scott's bilious eyes. His mind spun wildly. He grabbed hold of a lamp-post to steady himself and tried to think the thing out properly.

It must be a new building, that place—yes, that had to be the answer. He'd been doing a lot of desk-duties lately, after all. It was quite possible, what with new techniques and the speed of modern building, that the store had been put up in just a few weeks.

The place didn't *look* any too new, though . . .

Scott's condition rapidly grew worse—understandably in the circumstances, he believed—but there was a tube station nearby. He decided to take a train home. He usually walked the mile or so to his flat, the exercise did him good; but tonight he would take a train, give himself a rest.

He went dizzily down one flight of steps, barely noticing the absence of posters and the unkempt, dirty condition of the underground. Then, as he turned a corner, he came face to face with a strange legend, dripped in red paint on the tiled wall:

ROT THE TUBERS!

Deep creases furrowed the sergeant's forehead as he walked on, his footsteps ringing hollowly in the grimy, empty corridors, but his headache just wouldn't let him think clearly.

Tubers, indeed! What the hell—Tubers . . .?

Down another flight of steps he went, to the deserted ticket booths, where he paused to stare in disbelief at the naked walls of the place and the dirt- and refuse-littered floor. For the first time he really saw the *condition* of the place. What had happened here? Where was everyone?

From beyond the turnstiles he heard the rumble of a distant train and the spell lifted a little. He hurried forward then, past the empty booths and through the unguarded turnstiles, dizzily down one more flight of concrete steps, under an arch and out on to an empty platform. Not even a drunk or a tramp shared the place with him. The neons flared hideously, and he put out a hand against the naked wall for support.

Again, through the blinding flashes of light in his head, he noticed the absence of posters: the employment agencies, the pretty girls in lingerie, the film and play adverts, spectacular films and *avant-garde* productions—where in hell were they all?

Then, as for the first time he truly felt upon his spine the chill fingers of a slithering horror, there came the rumble and blast of air that announced the imminent arrival of a train—and he smelled the rushing reek of that which most certainly was *not* a train!

Even as he staggered to and fro on the unkempt platform, reeling under the fetid blast that engulfed him, the Tuber rushed from out its black hole—a *Thing* of crimson viscosity and rhythmically flickering cilia.

Sergeant Scott gave a wild shriek as a rushing feeler swept him from the platform and into the soft, hurtling plasticity of the thing—another shriek as he was whisked away into the deep tunnel and down into the bowels of the earth. And seconds later the minute hand of the clock above the empty, shuddering platform clicked down into the vertical position.

Ten-thirty—and all over Mondon, indeed throughout the length and breadth of Eenland, the lights went out.

Rosemary Timperley

SOME TRAVELLERS RETURN ...

IT WAS A WHITE ROOM. WALLS and ceiling were white. Furniture was white-painted. Curtains and bedspread were of plain white material. And the fitted, deep-piled carpet was like white close-cropped grass. On the white window-sill, in a white vase, was a bunch of white tulips. Their green stems and leaves provided the only colour in the room. Yet although all the room was white, there are different shades of white, so there was nothing monotonous about it. The painted sill, skirting-boards and furniture were gleaming white. Walls and ceiling were matt white. And then there were shadows, so that in places the whiteness turned to palest grey.

She stood there in her white summer dress and shoes, her white hair closely cropped and curly, and said: "It might have been meant specially for me. It's lovely. How much is it?"

He told her the rent. It was high, but worth it. Everything was so fresh and new. This all-white bed-sitter was quite different from the other fussy, fusty places she had seen. She decided to take it.

"Can you pay a month's rent in advance?" asked the landlord, pleasant yet businesslike: something solid and reliable about him.

"Yes, I can."

"Right. Let's fix it up then."

Within ten minutes she had given him a cheque for the rent, and been given in return a rent book, a key to the front door, and a key to the white room itself. Then he told her that she might move in as soon as she liked. He lived elsewhere so wrote down for her his address and telephone number and told her to get in touch if she needed help at any time. "Don't hesitate to contact me if anything goes wrong," he said.

Before she left, he added: "The upstairs rooms are still empty. I hope you shan't mind being alone in the house."

"Not a bit," she said. "I shall enjoy the quiet. I want peace." And she had no premonition that peace was the last thing she would find in this white room.

Two days later, she moved in with her few possessions. A natural loner, she always travelled light. As she unpacked, she kept glimpsing herself as she passed and repassed the white-framed mirror on the mantelpiece. Her own white dress and hair seemed to be at one with the room. She was white-hot with excitement at having found it, so much so that she felt rather strange and unreal, although it was all real enough.

Later she went out shopping. As the tulips had died, she bought some white roses—mad moment of extravagance—and bore them back in triumph. She let herself into the room—and received the shock of her life.

For someone was standing there.

A woman in black. Her long black cloak reached her ankles. Her long straight black hair fell almost to her waist. She was still as a statue and staring before her.

"Who are you? How did you get in?" gasped the new tenant.

"This is my room," was the answer.

"No. You've come to the wrong address. It's *my* room."

"I have been away, but it's still my room. I have the key," said the other.

"You must have been away a long time, seeing that it's all just been freshly decorated. Perhaps you didn't keep up with the rent. If you'd intended to come back, you should have told the landlord."

"How dared he decorate it in this garish, dazzling white," she said. "It used to be black. All black."

"Well, he obviously thought you'd gone away for good."

She turned aside for a moment and, with shaky hands, placed the white roses in the vase. "It's my room now. Please go," she said. And turned round again.

Already the other had gone.

She looked out of the window, expecting to see the black-cloaked departing figure. She saw no one. She went into the hall and listened, in case the other had gone into one of the empty rooms upstairs, but there wasn't a sound.

Returning to her white room, she saw with relief that there was a little white-painted bolt on the inside of the door. She drew it. At least that woman can't walk in on me while I'm here, she thought.

To steady herself, she made some black coffee, the first blackness which the room had seen—except for that woman—whoever she was—that previous tenant. She didn't eat anything. She had been eating less and less lately. Never felt hungry.

As the rest of the day passed, she began almost to forget about her visitor, but her unconscious mind must still have been very much occupied by her, for that night she dreamed of the room where she lay, and it was not white, but black. Black walls and ceiling. Black curtains and carpet. Black bedspread and sheets. She was herself lying in the bed, yet she was also that other, with long black hair outspread over the black pillow, and wearing a black nightdress. As can often happen in dreams, she had two identities: she was herself looking on, yet herself taking part. She was the other and the other was she. And she was terribly afraid.

The black door opened in the dream. Evidently there had been no bolt on it that other time. The black outline of a man, thickly black against the thin black air, approached the bed. She saw the blade of a knife flash silver in moonlight from the window. She felt its cold horror against her throat. And then there was a blaze of red before her eyes. She gave a choking scream—and woke.

The white room was back. She was entirely herself again, in her white nightdress. Terrified, because the dream had been so real, she got up and put on the electric light. She looked in the mirror. There was a faint red line across her pale throat, as if it had been gently stroked by a sharp blade which had caused little or no bleeding. Only the red line, marking where the lips of the trivial wound had closed. So the dream had been real, in its fashion. It had broken through some boundary and left a physical mark on her.

What had that knife done to *her*—the other one?

It took her all day to get over the horror of the dream. She went for a long walk in an effort to clear the fear. When she returned, she tensed herself in case the previous tenant was waiting in the room. But no. No one. She bolted her door—and dreaded the night.

However much you dread the night, there is no escape from it. Hours inevitably pass and shadows fall. The sky turns from grey to darker grey to black. She went to bed and lay wide-eyed, afraid to go to sleep. But one of the surest ways of going to sleep is to try to stay awake. Soon oblivion overcame her.

And the dream was back. It was a sequel, a continuation of the dream of the previous night.

She was again in the black room. The light was on. She was lying on the bed, blood still pouring from her throat. The man was busily cleaning blood off the black carpet. He made a competent job of it, and of his other cleaning operations—including removal of the blood-stained bedding and herself wrapped up in it. In stifled darkness, she was carried away—yet she was also watching herself being carried away. She saw him carry her out to his car and thrust her under the back seat. He drove out of town. He reached a wooded area. He lifted her from the car and laid her on the ground. He had brought a spade. He dug a grave and placed her in it. His movements were quiet, competent, unfussy. And all this time, she never saw his face.

As he flung the last spadeful of soil into the grave, she seemed to lose her watching self and be the other one entirely. She tried to cry out: "No—no—you've got the wrong one—I'm not dead——" All she managed was an eerie wail.

And her own cry woke her up, in the white room.

First—relief. Then—renewed horror. For she was not alone. The woman in the black cloak was standing by her bed. So she had not been murdered at all, as in the dream. And yet—she couldn't really be here, because the door was bolted. Only a ghost could have come through that door . . .

"You are not real. You are only a ghost." Who was speaking, herself or the other? The other vanished completely.

Now she went back over her nightmare, convinced again that her dream had been a record of that woman's murder, and that she herself had both watched it happen and been in the place of the victim. In dream, she had gone through the other's ordeal. Yet why? They were strangers. Because of the room, naturally. Or unnaturally. But then everything is natural if it happens. All is part of nature. But why had she become so over-sensitive to the atmosphere of the room? Common sense told her now that she hadn't been eating enough. People who go without food do have weird experiences. Shamans starve deliberately when they wish to contact the ghosts of their ancestors.

"Who were you, and who killed you by cutting your throat and then buried you in the wood?" she asked aloud.

Silence answered her.

She got up and drank black coffee. Still nothing to eat. Then she dressed to go out and tied a white scarf round her throat, to conceal the red mark which had become more conspicuous than it was the previous day. The word "stigmata" came into her head. Mind over matter in truth: dream impressing itself on flesh.

She went for a walk and bought a newspaper, something she did very seldom. Why had she done so today? She was soon to understand why. A headline stared at her:

WOMAN'S BODY FOUND IN WOOD.

She read that the body had been found by children after a picnic. Their parents had told them to bury their litter and they'd made a game of it, pretending that they were digging a grave. And they had hit upon the very spot where lay what was left of the body. It had been wrapped in decaying black sheets stained with old blood. It had been wearing scraps of black material which might have been a nightdress. It had long black hair. It had not been identified. Official surmise was that it had been there for two or three months.

What to do now? She imagined going to the police and telling her tale of seeing the ghost on two occasions and dreaming of the murder. She saw in her mind's eye the sceptical expressions that would flit across their faces, heard in her mind's ear the unspoken, "Oh, lord, another nut."

Then she remembered her landlord's saying that if she needed help, not to hesitate to get in touch with him. She went to a public call-box and dialled his number. He answered. She gave her name and added: "Please come. I need help."

He drove over in the afternoon, came breezing into the white room with that easy, businesslike air that made his presence such a comfort.

"What's up?" he asked cheerfully. "Lights fused? Plumbing gone wonky?"

"No, nothing like that. Something strange. Tell me, before this room was redecorated in white, was it all in black?"

"Yes. How on earth do you know that?"

"I had a dream—two dreams. Who lived here before me?"

He looked distressed, then shrugged his shoulders a little. "No reason why I shouldn't confide in you. It was my wife. We lived here together, in separate rooms. This was her room. She had it decorated in black because she said she was 'in mourning for her life'. That's a quote from one of Chekhov's characters.

She lived more in a world of fiction that a real one. She was—er—eccentric."

"And what happened?"

"She left me. Vanished without a word. I stayed on, wondering what to do, waiting for her to come back, poor crazy creature. She never came so I gave her up as a bad job. The place was getting me down, so I rented a flat out of town and decided to let the rooms in the house as bed-sits. I had this one done up first, in white, to banish that awful blackness. I hoped to drive away any dark atmosphere she might have left behind."

"Have you heard from her since?"

"Not a word."

"I think she's dead. Murdered. I've seen her ghost twice."

Silence. Then: "I think perhaps you're not very well."

"She was wearing a long black cloak and she had long black hair."

He nodded, his face turning pale. "She did dress like that, always, and she had black hair to her waist."

She went on quietly, with conviction: "I dreamed that I saw a man kill her by cutting her throat, then he buried her in a wood. And now she's been found. It's in today's paper." She showed him the newspaper article.

"Now that you've told me about your wife, and it's all fitted in with my visions and my dreams, I *shall* go to the police. Even if they don't believe me, I can't in all conscience do nothing. Will you come with me? You might be able to help with their enquiries——"

She stopped, for the man seemed to change before her eyes. His anxious, sensible, friendly face turned into a mask of cold determination in which there was no human compassion. He said, icily: "You, my dear lady, are too dangerous to live."

And suddenly it was as if the dream were back, but showing a face of reality. For it was really happening. She was just herself, not partly the other woman. The knife which flashed silver in the summer sun was a real knife. It came plunging down on to her throat, where already that thin red line awaited it, as she had taken off the white scarf earlier. For a brief moment she saw a blaze of red on the white carpet, and then the whole room turned red, as if painted in blood. Then the redness blackened. Dark. Darker still. Finally that spinning blackness from which, some say, no traveller returns. Yet some travellers do return . . .

It was a few months later when a red-haired woman wearing a red suit, warm against the chill autumn weather, came to look over a freshly decorated bed-sitter. It was a red room. Walls and ceiling were red. Furniture was red-painted. Curtains and bed-spread were of plain red material. And the fitted, deep-piled carpet was like red close-cropped grass. On the red window-sill was a bunch of red tulips . . .

"It might have been meant specially for me," she said. "It's lovely. How much is it?"

He told her the rent. She took the room. She moved in a few days later, unpacked her things, then went shopping. She bought some red roses, as the tulips had died. She let herself into the room—and someone was standing there.

A woman in white. White summer dress and shoes. White hair closely cropped and curly. She was still as a statue and staring before her.

"Who are you? How did you get in?" gasped the new tenant.

"This is my room," was the answer.

Ken Alden

JUSTICE TRESILIAN IN THE TOWER

THE GUARD LOOKED DOWN FROM THE battlement of the Well Tower at the three bears from the royal menagerie, who had been taken down to the Thames to catch their food. It was already so dark that he could only see them when they moved. As he watched, the white bear caught a large trout, put it into its mouth and began to shake it around. This was a mistake. The fish's flesh ripped and the bear lost its grip. The trout fell into the mud a few yards away, where it tossed and turned in agony. The bear moved forward to retrieve its meal, but the two pages who held its lead pulled it back.

"No, Titus!" shouted the larger of the two. "That one's for us."

The boy let go of the lead and tried to pick up the trout. Just as he was about to grab it, the bear growled and hit out at him with its paw. The boy pulled back, tripped over some driftwood and fell into the mud.

The guard heard footsteps coming up the tower's stairs. He turned to face the doorway just in time to see his sergeant come through it. He quickly came to attention and saluted. The sergeant did not bother to acknowledge this.

"Have you been given your instructions?" demanded the sergeant.

The guard nodded.

"The governor told you what the end result would be?"

Another nod.

"Then you should realise how important this is, and why it should look like an accident."

"My father and my father's father, my whole family have fought only for Bran. If I failed him they would kill me."

The sergeant frowned. "They wouldn't get a chance. We would do it for them."

The sound of laughter came up from the river bank. Both men looked down over the battlements to see what had happened. The page had now retrieved the trout. He was holding the twitching fish up in front of the bear and taunting the creature with it.

"What the hell are you doing down there!" shouted the sergeant.

The pages jumped and looked up at the tower.

"You should have brought those things in long ago. If you don't hurry we'll close the gates on you."

The pages glared at him for a moment. Then they started pulling their charges towards the steps that lead to the wharf.

"Leave the fish!" shouted the sergeant.

"But we can't just throw it away," protested the mud-covered page. "It's a good fish."

"Leave it or you don't get in."

The page dropped the fish and made a gesture at the tower. The sergeant had already turned back to the guard, however, and did not see it.

"Lieutenant Kinn is meeting him at the Lion Tower now," he said. "They should be here soon. Remember—he is powerful. His family could do us a lot of harm. So it must look like an accident."

"Yes sir."

The sergeant turned abruptly and started down the steps. When he was out of sight, the guard looked down over the battlement. The pages were now using the small bridge at the foot of the Well Tower to cross the moat. On the other side of the wharf the trout was writhing its last few moments away. The guard carefully noted its position. If he got this killing over quickly he should be able to retrieve that fish before the tide came in.

As the bears were led along Water Lane towards the Lion Tower, Lieutenant Kinn and Master Tyne stepped back into a doorway to avoid them.

"Those things have been involved as well," said Kinn. "On All Hallow's Eve, one of my men saw two of them on the casemate near the Brass Mount. When he threw a stone at them, they just disappeared."

"That sounds like a normal ghost," murmured Tyne. "Nothing out of the ordinary."

"Yes—well—a few days later another man was killed at his post by some wild animal."

"Um—I see." Tyne nodded his head a few times. "That does not sound like a normal ghost. I don't suppose there was any chance of something from your menagerie doing it?"

"None, they are too well guarded."

The men left the doorway and moved on down the lane.

"That's the Well Tower."

Kinn pointed it out. Tyne gave it only a casual glance.

"I hope you don't want me to spend the whole night up there in the fog," he said.

"Well that's where it always starts. What better place could there be to see it all?"

The lieutenant left the main lane and started to stride down the small path that led to the Well Tower. Tyne did not follow him.

"Wait!" he shouted.

Kinn came to a halt and turned to look at him.

"What's the matter?"

"You said there was plenty of time before it starts and I want to see the chapel first."

Kinn glanced at the tower and then reluctantly came back to Tyne. "It's this way," he said and he led Tyne through the opening by the Leathern Tower which took them into the great inner courtyard where the White Tower stood.

"Has it only been these floating things and beasts?" Tyne asked as they crossed the yard. "Nothing else?"

"There is nothing else that can be easily described."

"Well, so far you have told me nothing that would justify the fuss you are making."

"There are other things, but they are not material. It gets very oppressive here late at night." The lieutenant looked up at the stars. "Sometimes I think there is a huge ship up there, floating above us, in the darkness. The stars get blotted out and it is not by a cloud. There is often lightning when there is no storm."

Tyne nodded at the White Tower.

"Tresilian is in there, I suppose."

"Yes."

"Whereabouts?"

"His cell is at the top on the right."

"And the floating things always make their way to that part of the building?"

"Always—they go directly for the judge."

"Who was it suggested he be put there?"

Kinn shrugged. "Nobody, I think; he was just put there."

A raven landed on a nearby post and let out a squawk. Tyne stopped to look at it.

"How many of the birds are there now?" he asked.

"Oh, hundreds."

"And they are still fed?"

"That's the governor's orders."

Tyne went up to the bird and held his hand out to it. The bird jumped on.

"Your master is still as powerful as ever, then," he said to it.

The raven let out another squawk by way of reply and then flew off.

"Is the bird significant?" Kinn asked.

"Oh, very significant."

"In what way?"

"Let's see the chapel. Then I'll explain."

Kinn led him past the White Tower to the chapel of St Peter on the other side of the great yard. It was very near the homes of the mint workers' families, so there were a good deal of bones and other refuse scattered over the grass. Tyne kicked aside the decomposing head of a chicken.

"This is worse than Westminster," he said.

Kinn gave another indifferent shrug. "There are few dogs in the tower to clear it away."

They entered the chapel. There were only a few lit candles in it, but these were enough to show that the place was deserted. The two men picked up a candelabrum each and used them to illuminate the wall paintings. These consisted of demons, goats, sheep, oak trees, grape vines and many similar objects.

"How recent are they?" Tyne asked.

"Many come from the time of the Black Prince. But most were done just after Richard's coronation."

Tyne nodded his head several times. "Does the Bishop of London visit this place?"

"It's not part of his diocese."

"I doubt if he would be happy if he saw it anyway. You see that there?"

Tyne pointed at a naked man wrestling with a deer. The two figures seemed to merge into one so that the deer's antlers looked as if they were coming out of the man's head.

"That's Cernunnos. Some call him Herne. Now, you see that fellow there?"

He pointed at a man whose hair was replaced by leaves and who had a grapevine in his mouth.

"That's the Green Man of the May Day celebrations, and you see that dragon sitting on a globe? That's the Worm Ouroboros. They have merged ancient practices with the Bulgar, Albigensian, Catharist, Manichaean and Gnostic heresies. They are Lollards all right, and probably a lot more. You were right to bring me here. Your suspicions are well founded. Now let's have a look at the altar."

They walked quickly to the back of the church where a small wooden altar was kept. On the altar there was a Celtic cross and a small stone penis. Tyne picked up the penis.

"Few churches in London would openly display these now. Though I dare say that there are still several country churches who have them on the altar, rather than in it." He looked round at the walls again. "I'm surprised they don't have Shiela-na-Gig here."

Kinn looked puzzled. "Who?"

"Oh come, lieutenant, surely you have seen her carved in some church or other? She's that naked lady who sits with her legs wide open, showing all her charms. She's usually enticing her consort, Bal, the ever-upright. A well developed gentleman, that. You must have seen them.*

Kin shook his head. "I do not go to that sort of church."

Tyne grinned. "Ah—that's probably just as well. If you did you wouldn't have had to call me in. Now I don't suppose I could see Justice Tresilian, could I?"

Kinn looked unhappy about this. "What about the Well Tower?" he asked.

Tyne made a dismissive gesture. "Oh, there's still plenty of time for that. If I'm going to make a worthwhile judgement I'll have to see Tresilian sooner or later. There are no objections to that, I hope."

"I suppose not. But I'll have to arrange guards. We can't just walk in on him."

* *Historical note.* A survey carried out after the second world war by Professor Webb, then Secretary of the Royal Commission on Historical Monuments, showed that ninety per cent of British churches built before the time of the Black Death had a stone penis hidden in their altar. A good example of Shiela-na-Gig and Bal can be found at St Mary's Whittlesford, Cambridgeshire; it is by no means the only example though. Most areas have one or two; however, they are usually hidden away. The best know 'sexy' carving is the contortionist in Chalk Church, Kent; Charles Dickens mentioned it in *Great Expectations*. K.A.

Tyne strode towards the exit. Outside in the courtyard, he paused to let Kinn catch up.

"Wait here," said Kinn, when he did so. "I'll arrange for the guards."

He hurried over to the nearest house and began banging on its door. After about half a minute the bolts were pulled back and a unkempt youth stepped out into the courtyard.

"What is it?" he demanded.

"I want you to go to the Well Tower and fetch the sergeant and the private you will find there. Bring them to the northern entrance of the White Tower."

The youth frowned. "Why should I?"

"Because I am going to give you a groat, that's why."

Kinn fiddled around in his purse until he found an example of the coin. The youth examined it with distaste.

"This comes from the Bristol mint," he said.

"So? It's still legal tender. It does not have to be made by your fair hand. Do you want it or not?"

"All right."

"Thc Well Tower," Kinn reminded him.

"I remember."

The youth started to stroll across the yard.

"Run," Kinn urged.

He ran.

The lieutenant watched him for a few seconds, then made his way back to Tyne and the two of them headed towards the White Tower.

"You don't think it was King Richard who had those things painted on the wall, do you?" Kinn asked as they neared the tower.

Tyne shrugged. "Who knows if you don't? You're more likely to have some idea than I am. I doubt it, though. Richard—our sovereign lord, the second of that name—does not really oppose that sort of thing or support it. He doesn't really care. But there are a good many in court who do support it.

They may not do so openly, but behind the scenes that's a different matter."

"Who should I report this to, then?" said Kinn.

"Don't ask me. I'm just here to comment on the floating things." Tyne pointed a finger at the lieutenant. "You're the one who should know how things stand at court. If you don't I should find out who suggested that he be put in the White Tower and not one of the others. That would give you a clue."

"Why is the White Tower important?"

"Because it was built on a very ancient mound, part of an important pagan temple." Tyne pointed at the base of the tower they were approaching. "You can still see its outline, though the surrounding yard has risen over the years and partly masked it. Buried in that mound is the head of Brutis of Troy, the founder of London. Next to it is the head of the god Bran."

Tyne glanced at the lieutenant and saw only incomprehension in his face. "Really, my friend you show a most surprising ignorance. If you stopped any serf in the street he could tell you all of these things."

The incomprehension was replaced by annoyance. "I do not belong to the community of serfs, but to the pure community of God."

Tyne grinned again. "Yes, well, as I said before, that's to my advantage."

The frown deepened. "I would prefer less wit from you and more information. Tell me about this Bran."

The grin went. "He was an important god who ruled this island before the days of Christ. He could not be killed by any man. Or rather, he could only be killed by one who knew his real name. He always carried a twig of alder into battle. That was the clue to his name."

They came to a halt outside the White Tower's northern door. Tyne continued his lecture without a pause.

"A woman called Gwydion guessed what the twig meant. Shortly after Bran was killed when a poisoned arrow hit his heel. His head stayed alive though and kept on prophesying even after they had buried it here. The raven was his bird. It was his sacred symbol. That's why there are so many of them here. They are protecting him and carrying out his will. To a lesser extent, the crow, rook and the blackbird are also his."

"And you think that these people who want to harm Justice Tresilian still worship this Bran and so had him brought here, to the White Tower?"

"Possibly—Bran still has many followers in Essex and after the way the good justice treated Wat Tyler's colleagues, he would have plenty of enemies there."

The sergeant and the guard from the Well Tower appeared on the other side of the yard and started to hurry across it.

"This castle is part of a line of power," Tyne went on. "A line that greets the mid-winter sunrise. The two other sacred hills of London, Llandin and Penton, are also on this line. If you really want to know who is responsible for the flying things, you may find them there."

The sergeant and the guard reached the tower and saluted their superior.

"We are paying a visit to Justice Tresilian," Kinn told them. "You two will stand in for the White Guard."

He turned, pulled out a ring of keys and used one of them to open the tower's large oak door. Inside, there was a long stone corridor lit by only one burning torch. Lieutenant Kinn took this out of its holder and then led them along the corridor to a flight of steps. At the top of the stairs there was another corridor, at the end of which was Justice Tresilian's cell. Kinn got out his ring of keys again and pushed one of them into the cell's door. As the lock turned, there was a loud clang which was followed by a cry of fear inside the cell. Kinn then pushed open the door and held up the torch.

Tyne caught a glimpse of a thin old man with several days' growth of bristles on his face. Then Kinn entered the cell and blocked his view. When he entered the little room himself, Sir

Robert Tresilian was cowering on the floor, trying to hide his face in a corner.

"Come on—let's see you." Kinn gave the justice a kick.

The old man pulled himself further into the corner.

"Let's see you, I said."

He kicked again.

This time, the old man turned to look at them.

"He has the eyes of a statue," said Tyne after staring at Tresilian for a moment. "There is nothing there."

Kinn nodded in agreement. "I say that as well. But the governor is not so sure. The trouble is the good justice says so little that you can't really judge."

A strange noise sounded in the distance, something that Tyne had never heard before. He gave Kinn a questioning look.

"It's the elephant," the lieutenant explained. "It often does that when things start to happen."

"Let's get to the Well Tower, then." Tyne hurried from the cell.

"You two stay here," Kinn said to the sergeant and guard. "We'll certainly be back." Then he followed Tyne.

By the time both of them had reached the courtyard, every animal in the royal menagerie seemed to be giving voice to its fear.

"It's worse than ever tonight," said Kinn.

The two men hurried over to the opening by Leathern Tower. As they entered Water Lane there was a roll of thunder and a flash of lightning.

"That's how it always starts," shouted Kinn. "Look at the Well Tower!"

Tyne looked at it. The top of the tower was glowing slightly.

"That's the Roman's fire," he shouted back. "I've seen it on a ship's mast."

A ball of light left the tower and floated off over the moat.

All the animals in the menagerie suddenly fell silent.

"That's just lightning." Tyne went on shouting, even though

the noise was gone. "Just lightning—it's nothing supernatural."

Kinn started to hurry back towards the main courtyard. "Come here," he said as he ran.

Tyne followed him. As he left Water Lane, another ball of light formed at the top of the tower. This floated across the lane and hit Leathern Tower. There was a flash which dazzled Tyne for a moment.

"Follow me." Kinn ordered. "Follow me, or you'll miss it."

Tyne staggered after him and nearly hit a wall. By the time he had got out into the courtyard, another ball of light had formed. This managed to miss Leathern Tower and floated out over the courtyard. Behind it there was a thin trail of light, like a glowing rope attached to the ball. The other end of the rope was attached to the Well Tower. The further the ball got from the tower, the smaller it became. It seemed to lose its energy by creating the rope. Finally it disappeared completely and there was just the rope floating in the air.

"Is this how it always happens?" Tyne asked.

Kinn nodded. "Always. In fact, it's hardly started."

A new ball of light left the Well Tower. It travelled along the rope and when it reached the end continued onwards, leaving a new length of rope behind it.

"You see what it is aiming for, don't you?" Kinn shouted.

The ball was heading for the White Tower. It seemed to be aiming directly at the section which held Justice Tresilian's cell. About two-thirds of the way across the courtyard it ran out of energy and disappeared, leaving behind just the waving line.

"There's always a pause here," said Kinn. "I think it gathers up force for the final effort."

The line started to curl upwards. For a while, it looked as if it were going to try and tie itself into a knot.

Suddenly the elephant began to trumpet again. This was the signal for the whole menagerie to start howling.

"Look upwards," Kinn suggested. "Can you see the ship above us?"

Tyne looked upwards. All he could see was blackness. The stars had disappeared.

"It is only a cloud," he said.

"Look closely!" Kinn urged. "You can see the timbers of the thing."

Tyne could still see nothing.

Another ball of light started to make its way along the rope. This time, there was more force behind it. When it reached the end of the rope it sailed on until it hit the side of the White Tower. There was another flash, though not as dazzling as the earlier one had been. Tyne still hid his eyes. When he looked again the ball had gone. There was just the glowing rope rubbing itself against the stone wall.

Kinn ran towards the White Tower. Tyne quickly followed him. They both raced along the stone corridor and up the stairs. Kinn reached the top first and came to a halt there. The corridor that led to Justice Tresilian's cell was illuminated by the light that was shining through the cell's open doorway. The sergeant and the guard were out in the corridor trying to keep well back from the doorway and stare through it at the same time.

When he heard Tyne on the steps directly behind him, Kinn hurried forward again.

"Is it the same as before?" he asked as he neared the cell.

"Yes, sir," replied the sergeant.

Kinn stopped directly in front of the doorway and stared into the cell.

"Devil's work," he murmured.

The glowing rope had come right through the stone wall, apparently without damaging it. Once in the cell it split into several smaller strands that looked rather like the roots of a plant. Most of these roots had attached themselves to the walls and seemed to be discharging their energy into the stones. The biggest root, however, had attached itself to Justice Tresilian's chest and was causing him to jerk around like a fish out of water. His mouth was open, but he was apparently beyond screaming. The pain had made him lose all appearance of rational humanity. It had reduced him to mere twitching flesh.

Tyne did not hurry down the corridor. He strolled down it with an unnatural calmness. As he neared the cell, he gave a little nod. The guard then stepped forward and pushed Kinn into the cell.

The moment the lieutenant was in the room all the spare roots left the walls and attached themselves to him. There was another blinding explosion of light. This time, however, it lasted for over a minute. When all the energy had expended itself and the roots had faded, there were two inert bodies in the cell. The guard stepped forward and bent down over the one that had been Lieutenant Kinn.

"He should be dead," said Tyne. "It will look as if his heart has raced itself to a halt."

The guard moved over to the second body.

"He should be alive, though," Tyne added. "We can't have him missing his own execution." The magician turned to the sergeant. "I must get back to the temple immediately. There is still a lot to be done if we are to keep the force under control. You can tell the governor that we have got rid of his curious Christian."

Five days later the execution of Justice Tresilian took place. There was a huge crowd on Tower Hill. Practically everybody hated the justice. There had been singing and dancing for hours. But when the Tower's gates opened and the cart carrying Justice Tresilian was pulled up to the execution platform, everyone fell silent. They were silenced not by the sight of the justice, but by the large flock of ravens that flew above the cart. The few Christians who understood what this meant grew frightened. Many of them turned their heads away. Others started to hurry back to the city. Those who did not understand merely wondered what had caused such a flock to gather. The great majority of the crowd grinned, laughed and grew excited because of the sight.

As the executioners prepared the gallows the flock of birds grew bigger. All the crows, rooks and blackbirds of London were joining it, until there was a massive cloud of them, which cast a shadow over the gallows. When Justice Tresilian was pushed from the ladder and swung from his rope, a shout came from the crowd. Few were looking at the dying man. Everyone was staring upwards. At the moment the justice fell, the black mass up in the sky seemed to convulse and take on features. For that moment, there was a strange, unnatural, illusion. It seemed that up there in the sky was floating the huge detached head of a man. A man who was looking down at the gallows and laughing.

Author's note: Bran is a real mythological character. In fact, beyond the magic, everything in the story has a historical or mythological basis. The word "bran" means crow or raven and alder in various ancient British languages. He was one of the most important British gods, so important that King Arthur was said to have been jealous and had part of the Tower of London pulled down so that he could dig up Bran's head. Since the legend of the Tower ravens is still alive, he obviously did not succeed. The evidence for pagan survivals in this period is best presented in the work of Margaret Murray and Michael Harrison. Even some of the magic has a factual basis. In 1817 the Keeper of the Crown Jewels, who lived in the Tower, was at dinner with his family when a weird cylindrical object floated into the room. It was as thick as a man's arm and filled with a thick blue and white fluid which kept separating into thinner clouds. When something was thrown at it, the cylinder disappeared. Only a few months after this incident, one of the sentries died after being attacked by a huge phantom bear. Originally it was going to be Judge Jeffreys in the Tower. I naturally had an interest in him since the judge committed many of his worst crimes in Bridgwater and there is a remote possibility that I am descended from his chief executioner. However, I did not think that the story would really work in that period so I moved it back a few hundred years to the reign of Richard II. The case of Justice Tresilian almost exactly matches that of Judge Jeffreys. The Wat Tyler revolt that the justice helped suppress had many signs of a pagan uprising against the oppression of the church. K.A.

Les Freeman

MIND

FOR THE MAJORITY OF THE YEAR there was something special about Whitby, as far as Derek Benzies was concerned. It wasn't simply that the little fishing town looked majestic and steeped in history; it was the fact that it *felt* majestic and it *was* steeped in history.

On sharp icy days in December, when there was the threat of rain or snow, Derek would climb the one hundred and ninety-nine steps that led from the older part of the town up the steep cliff to the parish church and the ruins of Whitby Abbey. Once there, he could revisit the site of the old religious community, wander in the mystery of lost history, throw the odd copper coin—with a prayer to God or the devil—down the bottomless well that stood a few yards from the nave, before retreating to the shade of the still-used parish church to stare out to sea in the hope of spotting a storm arriving, or to watch snow clouds or snow storms battle their way across the bay and then shower the seafront with foam.

In the crispness of April he would wander through the shadows of the main street—only three or four yards wide—admire the stones that made up the old, stately, houses of Bagdale; take special note of the daffodils that held on to life in the old gardens that bordered the town centre; explore the eccentric museum and art gallery with the dull rays of the sun helping to illuminate exhibits; and then enjoy a fish lunch at the Angel hotel safe in the knowledge that, despite cod wars and fishing limits, that particular meat of the sea was good and fresh.

On the hot, claustrophobic days of August when Whitby changed itself from a town that traded with the sea into a town that took money from day trippers and holiday-makers, Derek rushed through the day with the speed of a young man frightened of growing old. He called on his clients—the few stores in the town prepared to sell expensive French silk clothing—and rushed out again to the more lucrative towns of Harrogate and Scarborough. There may be more money in those two towns, he told himself every August but in Whitby, when it was not overflowing with trippers, there was much more character.

He had been visiting Whitby and the rest of north Yorkshire for almost ten years, since he had gained an exclusive agency and had been determined to make it a success. And he had. There had been no question of him being replaced as long as his order book looked healthy, and, as the number of French silk dresses that turned up for official functions in the area testified, the health of that order book seemed assured.

Derek enjoyed his job. It meant that he saw some of the most beautiful countryside in England as he motored through the vast, almost unspoilt North Yorks Moors National Park, getting simple enjoyment from reading place names as varied and as unusual as Seave Green, Spauntan Moor, Rosedale Abbey, Goathland and Ugglebarnaby. But as much as he liked the sights and the sounds of the open countryside, his trips to Whitby, when they were out of season, were the highlights of his year. York and Harrogate, Middlesbrough and Scarborough may provide more orders; Whitby supplied more enjoyment.

It was December. So his Whitby visit was going to be something to enjoy. There was one major drawback—he had to get there and back by train. His car was out of action and the garage held out little hope of it being roadworthy within a week. But Whitby was a small town; and one of its main attractions was that it was best seen on foot. So a train journey was not going to spoil the trip.

The train from Middlesbrough to Whitby was a pay-train; a

green-backed diesel that snaked its way through the national parkland calling at thirteen or fourteen village stops before arriving at the sea more than an hour after starting its journey. His car could have done it in less time but, he told himself, by train it was more relaxing.

He arrived at Whitby in mid-morning; called on four shops and took four major orders; lunched on prawns and braised plaice and prepared to spend a couple of hours wandering and watching before catching the train home. It was cold and it was grey. There was a heavy sky that indicated to the knowing that snow wasn't far away. He tucked his scarf tighter inside the neck of his leather overcoat, and with briefcase wedged between his waist and his arm, sunk his hands deep into his pockets.

He glanced with little interest at the dusty antiques that stared out at him from windows of shops that were closed to customers until the summer; paid little attention to the other odd shops that offered products of Whitby's traditional jet industry. Instead he hurried along the twisting streets before climbing the one hundred and ninety-nine steps that led to the abbey. At the top of the cliff he stopped for breath. The silhouette of the abbey ruins greeted him; black and big and brooding. He paid his entrance fee at the gate and strode into the abbey grounds as the first flakes of snow fell and melted on the old stonework. It was cold. Very cold.

He stared up at the imposing, but empty, windows that had once risen in coloured splendour at the back of the altar, and he marvelled at the natural window pane of snowflakes that filled the empty spaces. It was as though someone had flicked flakes between glass in double-glazed windows and held the snow there for ever, moving in motion with the wind and the season. As Derek stared at the snow he saw that it was falling, actually falling and reaching the ground, only outside the walls of the abbey. There was no roof to protect the building and although he could look up and see the snow above him none reached the grass that made up the floor of the abbey. And while the grass outside the building was old and wiry and a dull dark green, the grass within the walls of the building was fresh and bright like grass in meadows at summertime. He shook his head to make sure he was still thinking straight, decided it was all due to the fact that the abbey's walls sheltered the interior of the old building, and marched out to the edge of the cliff to look at the sea.

The snow, however, was falling so heavily that it formed a thick blanket between him and the view. His hair was soon covered with whiteness while flakes that hit his coat were melting and sliding to the ground as water. He checked the time by the parish church clock and decided to head for the station, to miss his regular ritual of a monetary sacrifice to the abbey's well, but to give himself time to walk through the ruins again on his way back to the gate. He turned for a final view of the storm through the vast altar windows and saw that the snow was now falling on both sides of them and he was leaving a trail of footprints in the snow that covered the aisle of the old nave.

The train was at the platform when he arrived at the railway station and, after buying an evening newspaper he joined the train. He settled comfortably into the warmth of a non-smoking compartment and opened his newspaper. He couldn't read it, however, because of the shadows cast by the station roof. So he folded the paper and slotted it between himself and the side of the train, leaned back in the seat, and closed his eyes.

He didn't notice the train's engine start, and he didn't feel the train edge out roughly over the poor connections at the entrance to the station. He opened his eyes as the station was disappearing round a bend and the train was set straight for its last journey of the day.

Derek looked at the view. It was a habit he had whenever he travelled by train. He wanted to see the detail of the houses, the sidings, the farmscapes that other people would normally miss.

He wanted to spot the cracked windows in houses that looked otherwise architecturally perfect and well-maintained; he wanted to spot the stray growth of nettles or dock leaves in the cultivated gardens that backed on to the railway line; he wanted to spot the rogue rabbit or hare celebrating its freedom in fields normally reserved for barley or cabbages or corn. It wasn't the view as such that attracted him; it was the flaws in the view or the eccentricities of nature that he enjoyed.

He spotted the peeling white paint on a signal box as the train hurried by and he took particular note of the red scarf with white spots that the signalman was wearing.

Five or six minutes after leaving Whitby the train pulled into Ruswarp station. The honeysuckle that clung to the station walls was light brown and lifeless with touches of snow highlighting the line and the look of the plant which, in five or six months, would be alive again with greenery and heavy perfume and the hum of bees. The lettering on the station side needed some attention; the letter 'S' was slightly askew, and that would have to be straightened before the summer and the visitors returned. The train started to pull out of Ruswarp station; on the right, a tall grey flour mill that seemed to have stood on the same spot for centuries extended its shaft of shadow protectively over the village church. Both the mill and the church benefitted from the sprays of snow that clung to their roofs and windowsills, making them look cleaner, their lines more defined, their design more clear cut. They stood out defiantly against the blackness of the evening sky.

The train roared over a bridge that crossed the river Esk and Derek stared down at the ripples of water. He inhaled deeply, closing his eyes as he did so, and when he opened them again the train was pulling into Sleights, a small village warm and snug in a valley with rich farmland stretching up on both sides of it. The village Station Hotel backed on to the station and the hotel's garden stretched down to the platform. The garden was used by the customers when weather was good enough, and there were lupins and roses in the flowerbeds nodding their approval to hollyhocks stretching up to mingle with the branches of the apple trees. Apples were just starting to form and there was the merry chuckle of birds gloating over the discovery of young fruit.

On the platform Derek noticed a small huddle of children and a man. The man was about thirty-five to forty and the children—three girls and a boy—ranged in age from about four to twelve years. They were all well dressed and apparently well-behaved—until the train started to pull out of the station. As it did so, the youngest of the children, a little girl in a pink print dress with a white apron, exchanged her smile for a frown and screamed. The man bent down to console her but as he did so another young child—the boy—went through a similar experience and within seconds all four of them seemed to be wailing and crying and demanding the return of their mother who, Derek imagined, had boarded the train and was leaving the rest of the family behind. As he passed the family group he saw huge tears rolling down the cheeks of the little girl in pink and heard her crying out in a high-pitched voice: "Mummy, Mummy, please don't go." The man, presumably the father, dabbed her eyes with a handkerchief and Derek could read his lips as he explained that Mummy would only be away for a few days; she would be back very, very soon. But the little girl kept on crying and as the train got away from the station the cries of the children seemed to get louder rather than softer.

Derek smiled to himself as he remembered how his own two children could manage to cry at the least opportune times and, with the wailing still in his ears, he returned to his study of the details of the view: the branches in the trees; the birds on the branches; the feathers that made up the birds. He looked down and as he did so he saw the river rippling under a bridge, reflecting a blue sky. He sat upright, trying to check where the train was. And he recognised the views that heralded the approach of Sleights station. On his left was the booking hall and waiting room, over near the road was Sleights Station Hotel and at the back of the hotel was the garden alive with lupins and hollyhocks, stretching down to tempt train passengers at the platform. And there on the platform was the same small group of children and their father: four children—a young girl of about four in a pink print dress with a white apron, two sisters, a brother and their father. They were waving and kissing goodbye to a lady leaning from the doorway just ahead of him and as the train pulled away from the station there would be screaming, Derek told himself. The little girl would scream and then the rest would scream as well. He was right. There was a sudden wailing and weeping from the four of them as they stood on the stones of the platform; a great siren sound of crying; a great moaning that hit his eardrums like thunder; a wailing like a thousand cardinals bemoaning the death of a perfect pope.

Derek blinked and then stared hard at nothing. It was the second time he had seen the same view. The second time he had seen the same happening, from the same train. The same people. The same station. The same journey. It was impossible. Impossible for time to hiccough like that and give him a repeat performance of a ridiculous domestic scene.

He looked round to confirm his beliefs with fellow passengers, but the Whitby to Middlesbrough line is not a tremendously popular excursion in the middle of winter: there was no-one else in his no-smoking compartment. He stood up and saw there was nobody in the rest of the carriage. He slid the door of his compartment open and ambled through into the adjoining carriage in the hope of seeing the lady who was the cause of all the tears on Sleights station and to amuse her with the tricks that his brain was playing upon him. But that carriage was empty as well. He passed through it into the third and last carriage of the train; there was no-one in the second class area of the carriage and he felt his throat going dry as he looked into the first class compartment, knowing before he looked that the compartment too, was going to be empty. It was. Not even a ticket collector.

For a second or two he stood totally frozen, staring at the empty blue seats; then he turned and walked the length of the three carriages to check that he had not missed anyone. He hadn't. He sat down, trying hard to come up with a reasonable explanation and was suddenly struck by the idea that the lady in question could be at the lavatory. That would account for her not being in any of the seats; he had only looked at the seats. She could have put whatever luggage she had on a rack and then gone straight to the lavatory: hence the empty seats. Simple explanation. That was why he hadn't seen her. He would give her a couple of minutes and then take another walk down the train. It wasn't all that unusual for the train to be empty; that was one of the reasons why Dr Beeching had tried to close the line down in the early 1960s. But this was one line that had escaped the Beeching axe.

Derek leaned back in his seat with his eyes closed as the train ground to a halt. He kept his eyes closed. For some reason he could not explain he did not want to open them to check that this station was Grosmont, the third on the line towards Middlesbrough. He kept his eyes closed and ran over the list of orders in his mind that he had taken that morning. He thought about his lunch, about his climb up the one hundred and ninety-nine steps to the abbey; he remembered the snow that he had watched swathing the North Sea in cotton wool. He remembered the snow. The whiteness of snow. He opened his eyes and saw the garden of the Station Hotel at Sleights full of blue and crimson lupins, of lush green grass, and multi-coloured hollyhocks, poppies, roses and cornflowers. And there, less than a carriage-length away from him were the four children and their father going through the rituals of their goodbyes to their mother, to be followed by their sirens of remorse and their loud symphony of sadness. The train was pulling out; it was so soon after the goodbyes that there was not enough time for the woman to have settled her luggage and headed for the lavatory. Derek jumped from his seat and raced through the carriages, checking the seats, the signs on the lavatory doors, the luggage racks as he sped along the walkways. There was no-one there. No sign of anyone, either. No luggage; no engaged signs.

Finally he reached the first class compartment at the end of the train. He knew again that this time—like the first—it was going to be empty. It was. But as he stared at the twelve empty seats he suddenly gulped and found it difficult to breathe. The train was moving; there was scenery passing on each side of it, but there was no-one in the driver's cab. Nobody was driving the train. Nobody was guiding the train that insisted on calling at the same station time after time after time. He was the only person on the mad moving train. Then there was movement again in his body; he checked the driver's compartment a second time and then hurried back to his seat. The evening newspaper was still there, and his briefcase was exactly where he had left it. He put the newspaper inside the briefcase, strode out of the no-smoking area, and stood next to a door, fingering the catch and not totally sure of what was going to happen next. As he looked through the door window, the platform of a station came into view running alongside the door before coming to a stop as the train braked and halted. Derek cleared his throat and looked out.

It was Sleights. Again. The same pub was there, the same garden, the same station, the same four children, the same cries. The train shuddered as it prepared to leave again. Derek's hand flashed to the door. His fingers fumbled with the catch which refused to budge. He dropped his briefcase on to the floor as he did battle with the lock. Finally, growing more and more frightened, he flung himself at the door in his frenzied battle to get out. He landed with a thump on the station's cold stone platform.

"Hey, are you all right?" asked a gruff Yorkshire voice as a plump porter (the same man who acted as ticket collector—when there were any tickets to be collected—at Whitby station) bent down to check he was not hurt. "You came out of that door at a devil of a rush; it's a wonder you didn't break something. Are you sure you're all right?"

Derek stood up and straightened his coat.

"No. I'm fine," he said. "But where am I?"

"Where are yer?" repeated the porter. "Yer exactly where you were a couple of minutes ago—at Whitby."

"Whitby?"

"Where else?" asked the porter with a touch of suspicion.

Derek shrugged his shoulders and muttered that he wasn't feeling quite himself and willingly took up an offer from the porter of a cup of tea. In the porter's room Derek told what had happened on his train journey to Sleights.

"That's a very odd story you're telling," said the porter when Derek had reached his account of his escape from the train. "Very odd."

"Why?"

"Well, I'll tell yer if yer really want to know."

Derek nodded.

"Well," said the porter, "there are three or four minutes before the train leaves, so we're all right for time if I'm quick about it." He pushed his empty tea mug away from him. "It was last summer . . . it was very hot . . . that Mrs Martin from Aislaby Great Lodge had to go off to Middlesbrough to see her mother or someone who had taken ill. It was right in the middle of the summer holidays, so all her family was at home and it meant that Mr Martin had to stay behind to look after things. He called himself a farmer, but really he just used to sit at home and tell his men what to do. A Gentleman farmer.

"Anyhow, Mrs Martin caught an early afternoon train from Sleights—it would have been the 14.14, I think. Sleights station is just below Aislaby and after seeing her off Mr Martin was taking the children to Whitby Abbey because the eldest boy was writing something about it for a school project or something . . . it was all in the papers afterwards.

"Well, according to my mate at Sleights, the train arrived on time and left on time, but the children created all hell on the platform because they suddenly decided that they didn't want Mrs Martin to leave them. When the train pulled out there was much crying and screaming and scolding and slapping before they were all quiet. When they did settle down, Mr Martin's car is packed up with children and he pulls up the road, round over the big bridge and then up Sleights bank—it looked as though he was heading for the Guisborough to Whitby road. He could have gone through Ruswarp and up Ruswarp bank, but he didn't.

"On Sleights bank something went wrong with the car. And the next thing my mate knows is that the screaming and crying has started all over again, but this time from nowhere. Then the car skids all the way down the hill—backwards, and hits the bridge with such a bang that it's thrown up into the air and over into the river. All dead."

Derek gulped.

"And Mrs Martin?"

"Well," said the porter, "the people at the farm didn't really know where she was. They knew that she had gone home, but they didn't really know where home was. So it was late at night—after she had been to the theatre at Billingham—that the police finally got in touch with her and told her what had happened. And she took it very badly.

"How," asked Derek. "How badly?"

"Well," said the porter, "she never came back here again. She had to be looked after by her family and she was in such a state that she couldn't get back here for the funeral. Mr Martin's people were here, and the men from the farm, but not Mrs Martin. And after the funeral she took ill; really ill. She was so ill that she couldn't even get to Whitby for the inquest—

she was represented by a solicitor. She went into hospital and she's been there ever since. Doesn't know anybody now."

"Mad?"

The porter nodded sullenly. "And according to my mate from Sleights all she keeps talking about is saying goodbye to the children on the railway station, and then she hears them screaming and screaming—someone from the Great Lodge told him that."

Derek shuddered and asked the porter about the possibility of catching a bus to Middlesbrough, but when he was told he would have to wait an hour and the journey would be much longer than by train, he decided he had been merely subjected to a bad dream, strode back on to the train, buried himself in the *Evening Gazette* (which he could read because there were lights on in the train) and determined that he would forget all about the happenings at Sleights station the previous summer. There were four or five people in the carriage including an elderly lady in a black silk dress and old fur coat who was laden with shopping and who shared the no-smoking compartment with him. She smiled as he settled himself into his seat, and he threw a smile back at her plus a comment about the coldness of the weather.

Five or six minutes after leaving Whitby the train was pushing into Ruswarp station. The huneysuckle that clung to the station walls was light brown and lifeless with touches of snow highlighting the line and the look of the plant which, in five or six months, would be alive again with greenery and heavy perfume and the hum of bees. The lady in black dress and fur coat smiled her goodbyes as she gathered her bags and parcels together. Derek opened the compartment door for her, then, noticing actually how much shopping she was carrying, opened the carriage door as well and helped her out. He stood at the door for a second or two, watching her heading for the gate, and then returned to the no-smoking compartment and the shelter of his evening paper.

He checked the landmarks as they passed: the flour mill, the parish church, the bridge, the beginning of Sleights station. As he looked up to take in a full view of the station Derek saw that the whole carriage was empty, and although he remembered the train being warm at Whitby, it had now turned cold, terribly cold. He dropped his newspaper to the floor and listened to himself breathing deeply and felt sweat forming on his brow. He knew he was afraid, and was even afraid of admitting the reason for his fear. And then he gave a long, low, hollow, bewildered moan as he saw the garden of the Station Hotel come into view: it was lush green, with summer flowers tossing their heads to a summer sky. Derek leaped to his feet, grabbing his briefcase as he did so, bounded through the compartment and tried to open the carriage door which had been so easy to open only a few minutes earlier when he was playing gentleman to the old lady in the black silk dress and old fur coat.

As he touched the door the wailing began—like all the lost souls in hell demanding the attention of man. Derek's fingers started to bleed as he fought a losing battle with the lock on the door; he scratched and clawed at the window as he tried to pull it down to give him the chance of either opening the door from the outside or of leaping out. But by then the train had started again and was pulling away, past the children and their father. This time there was something unnatural about the four youngsters: they seemed to be grotesque plastic models, nothing real at all, with glycerine tears rolling down their cheeks and recorded screams coming from their mouths. It was an awful tableau that was infinitely more frightening than four young children simply crying after someone they loved. As he drew abreast of the group, all the faces turned in his direction, pressed their plastic noses against the moving window and screamed with horror directly at him, celebrating the fear they were creating in him. He drew back and covered his eyes and the train pulled out of Sleights station.

Derek licked blood from his fingers and then slowly did a

tour of the train. It was empty. No driver. No passengers. And the driver's compartment was as tightly locked as every outer door on the whole train. There was no apparent means of escape.

By the time he had finished his tour the train was pulling into Sleights station again. The screaming, which now seemed to be with him all the time, was harsher and louder and more deliberate—except for a brief spell when the train passed the group on the way out of the station, and all five of them turned to face him and, instead of crying out, they all laughed, their lips twisting into ghastly grins and grimaces as he shrank away from them.

After the train had pulled out of Sleights for the fifth or sixth or seventh time, Derek sat in his seat, cold and alone, trying to convince himself that he would eventually wake up. It was impossible, he insisted, for a human being to find himself locked in someone else's memory: in the mind of a mad woman. Impossible, he told himself as he looked at the screeching faces for the tenth or the twentieth time. Impossible to be locked in the mind of the insane.

But was he?

Mrs Martin was discharged from hospital early in January after doctors had said she had made an amazing and unexpected recovery. She no longer complained of living with the horror of her children's screams or the sight of their faces twisted in pain. She told her family that she would not like anyone to suffer the torments she had suffered, the horror of that terrible screaming, the anguish of those agonised faces; although she did confess, long afterwards, that in one of her saner moments in the month before she left hospital she had prayed to God or the devil to pass her misery on to someone else. Anyone else.

Derek Benzies?

T. H. McCormick

MORTON

Derek's story . . .

I DROVE AT AN EASY PACE.

No sense in flogging the Mini along.

It was a sunny, but cold March day: green buds on the bushes, and along the branches of the trees.

A good day.

My finals over and passed, one more year's work, and then . . . well, veritably, the world would be my oyster. I consulted the map, then stopped to check with the first person I met.

"The hospital? You're nearly there. First right, then straight on."

Going up the drive, I had plenty of time to study St Stephen's.

An old building, of dark grey stone. Probably built about the middle of the last century, with fanciful Victorian towers and parapets.

Not a glamour place, but it had four hundred beds, there would be plenty of experience, and it was only an hour and a half to London.

I went into reception.

"Hartley? Derek Hartley? You're in Mr Learmonth's unit, doctor. Wards 28, 29, 30. Sixth floor. You can walk up, or take the lift."

Going up the stairs, I noticed that the wards were named after famous surgeons—Treves, Wakley, Hunter, Macewen, Morton, Barnard.

Outside my ward was the name "Nathanael Morton",

together with the plaque of a severe-looking Victorian.

I started to familiarise myself with the place as soon as possible.

The three wards formed a surgical unit. Wards 28 and 29 were male. I was house-surgeon in 28; the corridor of 29 opened directly across from us, on the other side of the stair-well. Ward 30 was female, and reached by a long corridor at right angles to ours.

I settled in quickly.

The ward itself was the standard sort of place, long and gleaming, with vases of flowers. In the corridor outside were the usual places—sister's room, kitchen, linen room, sterilising and duty rooms.

I was kept pretty busy. The hospital had separate wards for heart, burns, kidney cases, etc., and we were doing general surgical work—fractures, car accidents, appendices, gall bladders, the lot.

It wasn't till a week later that I was walking down the long corridor that led to ward 30.

It was about half-past ten, and the whole place was quiet. No one else in the corridor, rooms empty, doors shut, lights out.

With one exception.

Halfway down the corridor, there was light coming from a large fanlight above a door. A very strange sort of light, I thought. Not the usual sort of thing, from the large globes in the hospital, but yellower, and much softer.

I approached it, and then . . . Oh God, not this, I thought.

I could feel myself starting to shake, my legs weakening. I knew that unless I got away, I'd be physically sick.

I moved back a few steps. Still the nausea.

Whatever had happened in that room, had been bad, bad.

I've always had this abnormal sensitivity to people and places. I don't know what it is, or why I have it. "You're receptive to the aura," a spiritualist once told me.

Four years ago, I was looking through a flat I thought I

might rent. I couldn't go in one room, I felt so affected. At the house agent's they told me that the previous tenant had murdered his wife there, in a drunken quarrel.

A couple of years before that, I'd been out in Derbyshire on a holiday tour, with a group of industrial archaeologists. I felt the same atmosphere in one of the places we visited, though there seemed no reason for it. Some time later, a man was arrested. He'd murdered his girl-friend, climbed over a barbed-wire fence, and thrown her down the mine shaft we'd just been looking at.

And now this . . .

Then I steadied myself. Damn it all, I might be imagining it.

I looked at the door.

A heavy, old-fashioned one.

I stepped forward, and turned the handle.

Locked.

I turned at the sound of footsteps in the corridor. The little Welsh nurse from ward 30.

"What's the matter, Derek? You look as if you'd seen a ghost."

"That light," I said. "What do you make of it?"

She stared. "What light?"

"There," I said, pointing. "Above the door."

She looked upwards, her forehead creased.

"I certainly don't see anything."

We stared at each other. I felt that coldness again. "Well . . . I . . . come and stand where I am."

She did so.

"That room's in darkness," she said. She tried the handle. "And anyway, it's locked."

I mumbled something about being mistaken, an odd trick of the light, and she went on to my ward.

I took a few steps along the corridor, and looked back.

The light was still burning.

I tackled the ward sister about it, next morning.

"What's that room along the corridor?"

"Which one?"

"On the way to ward 30."

"Oh. That one." She looked vaguely embarrassed. "I think it's supposed to be some sort of spare room."

"Spare room!" I said. "We're crying out for space."

"Well, it's empty now." She waved her hands expressively. "You know how it is. Some places just never seem . . . suitable, for anything. I believe they tried to use it two or three times, as a store room, but it proved unpopular, somehow." She paused reflectively, for a moment. "Maybe you'll find something about it in a history of the place. I believe it was originally used by Nathanael Morton."

"Who?"

She laughed. "Morton. The man this ward is named after."

We had a common lounge, for the resident house-men. Well-furnished, comfortable, with a surprisingly good library.

I started looking through its reference section.

I was lucky. They had Hyamson's *Dictionary of Universal Biography*.

I flipped through the Ms. *Morton, Nathanael, Eng. Surg; 1837–1871.*

Not much there.

A note beside it said that full details would be found in the *Concise Dictionary of National Biography*.

That would have to wait several days, till I could get down to the local library.

I looked at the entry again. Only 34 when he'd died. Now, what had happened there?

"What are you looking for, Derek?" someone asked.

I told him.

"Morton? Why not ask your chief?"

I struck my head reproachfully. "Of course."

The chief was pretty decent—very decent, in fact, compared with some I'd worked under.

At eleven o'clock, after we'd done the ward rounds, we gathered in his room, and started on coffee and biscuits.

He offered me a cigarette.

"I thought you'd have given them up, sir," I said.

He laughed. "Cigarettes are like anything else. There's nothing wrong with them, in moderation."

We chatted for a while, then, "There's one thing I was wondering . . ."

"Yes?"

"About this ward. Who was Nathanael Morton?"

"Ah . . . yes . . ." There was silence for a moment. "It's not something we're too proud of." He turned towards his desk. "Just a minute, I think there's a history of the hospital . . . Yes, here it is."

He handed it to me.

It was open at the reproduction of a Victorian group photograph.

A surgeon facing you, in his white operating gown; left hand grasping the right, in which there was a scalpel.

Another man beside him. Six nurses.

It was the surgeon who dominated the group.

A man who found it difficult to relax and be pleasant. Tall, lean-faced, the jaw set and determined, and, above all, the eyes.

Those eyes! Even in the photograph, you could feel the fanaticism behind them.

"So that's him?"

"Yes." He motioned me to keep the book. "It's really a matter of what I was saying earlier, about moderation. Morton? He was a brilliant surgeon. Brilliant. Died in 1871."

"I know."

"He specialised in heart work. Pioneered some new techniques that are still in use. He knew he was good, and felt he was on the verge of greater things. He became convinced of it, and then," he shrugged, "it became an obsession. He came to believe that he was justified in whatever he did."

"But what *was* he doing?"

"Heart transplants."

"For God's sake," I exclaimed. "In 1871!"

"Yes," he nodded. "They'd been thought of by then, but only as the wildest theory. Morton hadn't the equipment needed, no transfusions, or drips, or idea of aseptic technique, and anyway, his ideas were all wrong. Really, it was just murder."

"But . . . didn't anyone realise what he was doing?"

"His staff did, but they believed he was on the verge of a great break-through, and kept their mouths shut. After all, in his own wards he was supreme."

I was still puzzled. "What about his superiors? Surely they must have realised?"

"They knew he was doing heart operations, all right, but they didn't realise he was attempting transplants." He drew on his cigarette. "Eventually rumours began to circulate, and the police made a raid, just when he had started an operation."

"What happened?"

"He was so distraught, or enraged, that he killed the patient. Anyway, he was tried for murder, and hanged."

"Fantastic," I muttered. "Wasn't he mad?"

"No," he said, "just obsessed." He stubbed out his cigarette, and we stood up to go. "Of course, these used to be his wards," he said casually. "And you know that room round the corridor, the one with the fanlight?"

I nodded.

"That's where he did his operations."

Knew it, I thought triumphantly, *knew* there was something wrong with that room.

So it went on for a couple of months.

Two or three nights a week, the room would be lit. When I could, I listened. At first I thought there was nothing to be heard, then I wasn't so sure. No voices, but an occasional sound like the rolling of a trolley, or the clink of instruments in a bowl.

I daren't listen too much. Already I was aware of some curious glances, gossip. Much more, and they'd be thinking I was round the bend.

Then we got a new houseman.

We were giving a farewell party for Nazir, who was going back to Pakistan, and I was introduced to him.

Typical Celt. Small, dark-haired, wiry. Looked as if he'd make a good addition to our rugby team.

We shook hands.

"Angus Mackinnon," he said.

"Let me guess," I replied. "You're from the Highlands. And Glasgow University?"

He smiled. "From Skye. Then on to Edinburgh."

"Play any rugby there?"

"Only for the second fifteen."

"That's good enough for us. And if you break a leg, playing . . ."

"Yes?"

"There'll be plenty of doctors in the audience."

He fitted into the place quite well, and was quite popular. "Quite." He was friendly, yet there was always something apart in him, something of the cat that walked by itself.

I wondered . . .

I heard, too, that one evening they'd been fooling about with a ouija board in the residents' lounge, trying to contact the spirits. He'd refused vehemently to have anything to do with it.

"Seemed terrified," I was told.

A few weeks passed, and I had half forgotten it.

The daily routine kept us busy enough. Tagging along after the chief on his rounds, X-rays, blood tests, checking the treatments that people were getting, and writing reports.

Then, one evening, we left the ward together for our supper break.

I glanced involuntarily at Morton's room, as we started down the corridor, but it was in darkness.

We were hurrying past it, when Angus suddenly stopped as if he'd run into a brick wall.

He gripped my arm.

"God save us, what's in there?" he said jerkily.

"Why?"

He was white, shaking.

"Thon's not a canny place," he said, "I can feel it. There's been something very wrong in there."

"Thank God for that," I said.

He stared at me. "What do you mean?"

I told him what I'd felt about it. The noises I thought I'd heard. The light I'd seen.

"And no-one else saw it?"

"No."

"You're psychic, of course," he said. "Where something very good or bad has happened, it leaves vibrations, which can be picked up by those who are sensitive enough. What has happened here has been evil."

"Even the others don't like the place," I said, "but the atmosphere almost overwhelmed you."

"I was always that way." He smiled weakly. "People laugh at superstitious Highlanders with second sight and all that, but it's not a thing to joke about."

"That's why you wouldn't use the ouija board."

He nodded his head. "I never tamper with the supernatural. I'm too afraid of it."

"Christ!" I said, "I'm getting tired of this. Here I am, creeping about, afraid of . . . what? All right, every time I've had this feeling before I've been justified, but couldn't I be imagining it, this time?"

Angus smiled sardonically.

"Who are you trying to persuade? Remember, I felt it too, and I knew nothing about all this till you told me."

"Let's get the key, and go in," I said.

He looked at his watch, and shook his head. "Too late. We'll have to bolt our supper, as it is."

"How about tomorrow night?"

"Done."

We left the ward together.

"Got the key?" he asked.

"Yes."

He had a torch in his hand. One of those damn great heavy ones, about a foot long. "Thought it might come in handy," he said. "How about you?"

I drew a truncheon from my pocket. "I borrowed it from a bloke in Security Express."

We hesitated at the door. Then, "To hell with this," I said, and turned the key in the lock. We stood together just inside the door, and Angus flashed the light round.

Nothing.

It was a large, empty room, with a skylight occupying most of the ceiling. The walls were white-tiled, and against one of them stood an old-fashioned operating table.

"Operating room," I said. "Come on."

Two smaller rooms opened off it. They were also empty. "Where they scrubbed up," Angus said. He ran his finger along the inside of a sink. "No dust."

"The cleaners do it once a week," I said. "Always two of them. They won't be left alone in the place."

We went back into the main room, and paused at the door. Angus swept his torch round the room again.

There was a sense of anti-climax.

"Looks like a wasted evening," I said.

"There's something about this room," Angus said, "but it's not here now . . . Let's go outside, and look up at it. We may see something we hadn't noticed before."

We went into the grounds, and I looked at my watch. Just after eleven. Rows of windows, almost all dark. An occasional faint gleam from a shaded ward lamp. Here and there, the blaze of light from a kitchen.

We stood back, and looked up to the sixth floor.

As we did so, that yellow light came on again.

Angus gripped my arm. "Come on, Derek."

We raced up the stairs, one flight after the other, and stood panting outside the door. The fanlight was still lit. We looked at each other. Now we could both *feel* something inside.

"What'll we do?"

Angus bent down, and put his eye to the keyhole—something so obvious, of course, that I hadn't thought of it before.

"What is it?"

He straightened up slowly. "Gaslight," he said incredulously. "There are four of them on the right-hand wall."

"Gaslight!" I exclaimed. "This bloody building's all-electric."

"Aye," Angus said slowly, "but how far back in the past do you think this scene is, that we're seeing now?"

"Look again," I said. "Is there anything else? Can you see anyone?"

He bent down.

"No, that's all." There was a pause. "The jets are enclosed in glass holders," he said. "They look Victorian, to me."

"They would be. About 1871, I bet."

"Morton?"

"Who else?"

We looked at each other. "To hell with it," I said, "I'm going in. Give me the key."

I put it in the lock.

Immediately the light dimmed, and went out.

I opened the door, and swept the torch round the wall where the jets had been.

There was nothing there.

But this time we encountered something. A presence in the room trying to force us out, as palpable as a hand thrusting against your chest.

It was Morton, all right.

You could *feel* it, the power of that will, the implacable determination that his wishes should be carried out, a psychic force that was malignantly alive.

Get out, it screamed, *get out*, GET OUT.

"The other rooms," Angus panted.

"You know there'll be nothing there."

"Come on."

They were as bare and empty as before.

We got out of the place with a rush. As we stood against the wall gathering our breath, a nurse passed us, gingerly carrying a couple of wet X-ray plates. "Have you two been in there again? It must be a fascinating place," she said sarcastically.

We couldn't be bothered to answer.

Angus looked exhausted; I don't suppose I was any better.

"It's getting a lot worse in there," I said.

"Yes," he agreed wearily.

"You think it's Morton?"

"Of course. Who else could it be?"

I remembered something that had been puzzling me. "Why do we only see this light occasionally?"

"Well, he only operated on some nights."

I stared at him.

"You think that's what he's doing now?"

"That's my guess." He looked embarrassed. "I think it's some sort of re-enactment of what happened in the past."

"Why the hell should we have to go skulking past this place? Why don't we do something about it?"

"Such as?"

I hesitated. "Well . . . exorcism? Don't the Anglicans and Catholics have services for it?"

"I don't know," he said doubtfully. "It's possible, I suppose. Still . . ." He paused.

"Well?"

"We could keep quiet about it," he said slowly. "We know what's in there. As for the others . . . you heard that nurse.

They think we're either stupid, or going a bit crazy."

"I think it should be faced out," I said. "After all, what can these ghosts, or whatever they are, actually *do*? We've felt something. Maybe we've heard something. But we've never actually seen anyone."

"That's so," he agreed cautiously.

"I'm going to put it to the test," I said. "I'm off duty on Friday. I'm going to spend the night there. With your torch, and my truncheon, I'll be O.K., and if any of the others are thinking of trying any tricks," I clenched my fists, "they'll be very sorry indeed."

"Wait till next week, and we'll both do it. I'll be off, too."

I shook my head. "No, now's the time." Then I paused. "Just one thing, Angus."

"Yes?"

"You'll keep an ear open for anything?"

"Don't worry. One shout, and we'll all be there."

Angus's story . . .

The plan was all right.

Derek would stay in Morton's room, and I would be up and down the corridor frequently.

Unfortunately, we forgot what can happen in a hospital.

We had a haemophiliac in the ward, and he started bleeding. I got the equipment for a transfusion set up, swabbed his arm, and slid the needle into his vein.

Or tried to.

I tried it six times, with the sweat growing colder on my forehead and body.

It was a tricky situation. He was going into a state of shock, and the vein was collapsing, making it even more difficult to get the needle in.

"All right," I said, "we'll cut down on a vein in the foot. That should be easier." I told the nurse to get a tray ready, then ring the S.H.O., and ask him to come along.

No use standing on your dignity, when someone's bleeding to death.

The senior house-man arrived.

"What's the trouble, Angus?"

I told him.

"Hmm," he said. "Not too good. Try and get the needle in, again."

I took it in my hand, bent down wearily, and it slid straight in.

I straightened up triumphantly. "Now, how's that for . . ."

Then it started.

A high-pitched scream of fear, repeated again and again.

"What on earth's that?" the night-nurse gasped. "Where's it coming from?"

But I was already running down the corridor.

The light was streaming from the fanlight above the door. Now the screaming changed to a gurgling, choking sound, and lessened in volume.

"Derek," I shouted. "Derek!"

No answer.

The door was locked. I stood back, and charged it. The result was agonising; it might as well have been made of iron. I raised my foot and started kicking frantically round the lock, even though I knew it was equally hopeless.

There was the sound of feet, and the nurse came running down the corridor. Other feet too, voices, then some more nurses and a couple of porters appeared.

The night-nurse reached me first.

"The axe, doctor. Try the axe."

I looked round. There was one in a glass case on the wall. I put my fist through the glass, and seized it.

I went at the door like a madman, panting, shaking and cursing, as I smashed at the panel above the handle.

At last it gave.

I put my hand through, turned the key from the inside, and burst into the room.

Even though I had half expected it, it was bizarre.

There they were, grouped round the body on the table, in the clothes of a century ago; the nurses in black dresses, and close-fitting caps with long white streamers, the two men with operating gowns over their morning coats.

One held an old Schimmelbusch mask over Derek's face, and was pouring some liquid from a dark brown bottle over it. The air was heavy with the sickly-pungent smell of chloroform.

Morton was bending over the table, with a scalpel in his hand.

They seemed to be unaware of anything, until the door burst open.

I was in front, blocking the view from the others, and was the only one who could see what happened, although later it all appeared so fantastic . . .

Morton straightened up, and there was a look of absolute fury on his face.

The knife slashed downwards.

And even as it did, they started to fade.

How can I explain it? You switch off an electric fire, the elements slowly darken; you turn off the current to a valve radio, but you still hear the sound for a few seconds.

So they—spirits, ghosts, revenants, whatever they were—became wraith-like, dimmed and dwindled.

In five seconds they had disappeared, and there was nothing left in the room.

Nothing except the old-fashioned operating table, and the body on it, and the blood dripping from the great gash in its throat.

Eleanor Inglefield

THE SINGING STREAM

I CAN REMEMBER THE TIME WHEN the road was nothing but a planner's dream. The time when the roads of Cornwall were still gentle and winding and the hedges that bordered them were still full of flowers. Even when the rest of England was suffering motorway madness, Cornwall still retained her individuality, as a place where people came for rest and relaxation. I am old now but I can remember it all beginning. Looking back I find dates confusing but the events that took place on those dates still stand out in my mind.

When I was about fourteen there was a comet, and as the rumours about the motor road began to circulate about that time, I decided in my mind that the comet was in some way responsible for the disaster. Dad had a telescope on the flat roof of our house and one morning before daybreak he came and woke me, and together we crept up on to the roof and we peered in turns at the comet that looked, for all the world, like a flaming torch riding high above Cowper's Hill.

When I went to pay my weekly visit to Mrs Tyack I told her about the comet. I was very excited about it but I remember my old friend was rather silent. We were rather proud of Mrs Tyack—she was our local celebrity. She had come to us from Switzerland. In her heyday she had been a brilliant scientist but a climbing accident resulting in brain damage had put paid to her career. So, putting her past behind her, Mrs Tyack—she would never be called doctor—returned to the land and county of her birth. Here she lived aloof and fiercely independent with only Polly Trebilcock, her devoted daily, to attend to her wants.

At first, people tried being kind and neighbourly but she repulsed all well-meant advances. Her pride suspected pity and she resented it, and by and by people learned to leave her alone.

My twin brother Peter and myself were the only two people who found any welcome at Willow End. It all started the day we found her wandering in one of her memory lapses, during which she was totally lost, and, knowing her by sight, we took her home and did our best to reassure her. As Polly Trebilcock wasn't there I made her a cup of tea, while Peter talked cheerfully about his rabbits and any other mundane thing that came into his head that he felt might calm her bewilderment. After that, we had entry to Willow End and, as I remember, took full advantage of the privilege. It was usually a Sunday afternoon when we made our weekly visit and Polly, who did a Saturday baking, always left a small mountain of cakes for our delectation. This custom we kept up till Peter went to boarding school, after which I made the visit alone. To my intense disgust I had been made to remain at home and share the vicarage governess.

One day—it was some time after the comet—I found Mrs Tyack in her sitting-room with an odd looking map spread out on the table before her. It was a map of Cornwall and it was covered by a fine network of lines. It looked for all the world as if a spider had woven a net across it.

"What are those lines?" I asked curiously.

Mrs Tyack said nothing for a moment, then she said, "I couldn't sleep last night, had odd dreams. I do sometimes, it's nothing new but they made me remember this map. I drew it years ago when I was in Switzerland."

"But what do the lines mean?" I persisted.

Mrs Tyack smiled and said, "About a hundred years ago there lived here in England a man called Alfred Watkins. Does the name mean anything to you?"

I shook my head.

"Well, it's not really surprising. Even in his own day he had a limited following. His father had a large wine and spirit business in the south of England and young Alfred acted as his travelling representative. Alfred's interests being largely antiquarian, he managed during his travels to visit a great many churches and ancient sites, thus combining business with pleasure with a certain amount of success. One day he was standing on the Bredwardine Hills and suddenly he had a vision. It seemed to him that he saw below the surface of the landscape and it was as if, to quote his own words, 'the ground had become transparent' and he saw a web of lines linking the sites of antiquity. In short he saw in his mind's eye a vision of prehistoric Britain and a mystery that civilisation had lost. Alfred Watkins lived to write two books, *The Old Straight Track* and *Early British Trackways.* I found both of them in the English section of a Zurich Library and I remember with what excitement I read them. I sent back to Cornwall for a local map and set about finding the lines between the various sites and monuments—and this is the map."

"Did you dream about the lines?" I asked, after a pause.

"Not these lines," said Mrs Tyack, "what I dreamt about were the fault lines. They lie all over the world. There is one here running straight as an arrow over Dartmoor and down towards Lands End." Then, seeing my bewildered face, she laughed and said, "Fault lines are cracks along the magnetic current that covers the surface of the earth," she said. "When that happens the magnetic current becomes violently agitated and causes turbulence, and now they are planning to extend one of their horrible motorways right along the fault as far as Lands End."

"I know," I said, "Dad was talking about it the other evening. He said it will bring increasing trade into the county."

"If they build this road they will bring a good deal more than trade," said Mrs Tyack grimly.

"What do you mean?" I said, rather uneasily.

"Have you never read about motorway madness?" said my

old friend, turning her rather wild blue eyes in my direction. "Have you never heard about hundreds of car drivers apparently going mad on these motorways and driving at high speed to obvious destruction? That occurs when the motorway touches a section of a fault line. I have another map here showing the principle lines and where they intersect with the roads. In all cases they cover what are known to the authorities as accident black-spots."

There was a longish pause after that. Then Mrs Tyack deliberately rolled up the map and, getting up, put it away in the bottom drawer of her writing desk.

"When they do build this road," she said coming back to the table, "Willow End will be right in its path."

"I expect it will be years before they begin it," I said, trying to comfort her, "the county council are still arguing about planning permission."

Mrs Tyack said nothing and together we sat at the window looking out at the shining river on the far side of the road, with its dart-shaped flock of low-flying birds making for the estuary mouth which they did every evening in order to nest in the high cliffs. At daybreak, the flight was in reverse as they swept down river again to the feeding grounds. What would happen to all this peace if the threatened motor road was cut through the heart of Cornwall? Would Willow End really be ruthlessly swept away?

"Couldn't somebody tell them?" I said rather desperately.

Mrs Tyack said coldly, "Somebody could, if they wanted to be branded as a lunatic. No, dear child, they will build their road and nothing can stop them, and as a result hundreds are destined to die—and there is nothing you or I can do about it except pray. I am an old woman and you are only a girl. Better forget this whole conversation. Now run along home, it's beginning to get dark."

All the same, I couldn't forget that conversation and at supper that evening I asked Dad if he had ever heard of Alfred

Watkins.

"I don't think so, what has he done?"

"He lived about a hundred years ago," I said, "he was a wine merchant by trade and wrote a book about the lines he saw stretching from one prehistoric site to another."

"Sounds an eccentric to me," said Dad, "they do crop up from time to time. Where did you hear about him?"

"Mrs Tyack was talking about him this evening."

"I'm not at all certain you should go so much to Willow End," said mother fussily, "that woman strikes me as decidedly unbalanced. I'm sure she's not a wholesome influence on a growing girl."

"There's no harm in Elizabeth Tyack," said Dad unexpectedly, "I knew her people when she was young. Her father was Abel Sampson, they had a large farm between Penzance and St Ives. I remember when Elizabeth won her scholarship to Oxford. She had a wonderful brain. That accident she had was an absolute tragedy!"

When Peter got back from school for the Easter holidays I told him all about Alfred Watkin's leys, as Mrs Tyack had taught me to call the lines, and together we pored over her map of Cornwall, discussing with fervour and at great length the possibility that a motorway built straight down a fault line might prove to be a killer. Improbable as it might appear to the mature, we were at the age when the theory was utterly fascinating. Oddly enough, having been instrumental in propagating the idea, Mrs Tyack seemed to take no further interest in the subject, though she tolerated our endless speculations. I think perhaps it amused her to listen to us arguing.

It was a year later when we heard that the plan for the road had reached the stage of serious consideration and shortly after that the plan was approved and accepted by the Cornwall County Council. One or two of the older members had died and another couple had resigned and the power had now passed into the hands of the so-called progressives. When Mrs Tyack heard that the plan had been passed, she said quietly, "Well, I suppose it's inevitable. If it doesn't come now it will come in the near future. One can only hope things don't turn out as badly as I fear they might."

She was pleased, I think, when I told her that Dad had been against the scheme from the beginning. "I'm not surprised," she said, "I remember your father when we were both young. He was never one to go along with the crowd. I hope you two will take after him. If you do, you will usually find yourself on the opposite side of the fence to the mob. It can be a lonely position but people who do that usually get things done in the end."

"Did you?" I asked her directly.

Mrs Tyack laughed and said, "Usually, Paula, usually. I fancy I wasn't altogether easy to work with." Then she got up and going to the window stood looking out towards the river on the far side of the road. Presently she said, "In a few years this tranquillity will have gone for ever."

Something in the way she said it made me feel uneasy. "You mean they *are* going to pull down Willow End?" and I said, hesitatingly, "You mean they are turning you out, already?"

"Not officially, but it will come," she said grimly, "and my home won't be the only one."

I went home feeling rather depressed.

It all happened very slowly. I was in my first year at Exeter University when the road first touched Cornish soil. Driving home for weekends I found myself shuddering at the sight of the massive upheaval that attended the birth of the monster that was supposed to bring such economic growth to our beloved county. True, our sideroads and lanes remained comparatively untouched, and I made a point of travelling on them whenever I could. When I got back for my first vacation, Dad told me that Willow End had at last been scheduled for demolition and Mrs Tyack had been given notice to quit.

"But what will happen to her?" I asked in panic.

Dad said, "I don't know, Paula, that is what is worrying me. As soon as I heard about it I went down to see her. Rather to my surprise, she asked me in. I offered her the farm cottage near the Long Acre. She thanked me but said she wouldn't be needing it. I asked her if she had other plans and she said with a little smile I didn't altogether like, that she had. Then she said something that made me very uneasy. She said, 'They can build their road but it will be over my dead body.' I came home, I assure you, in a very unhappy frame of mind."

"When did this happen?" I said after a pause.

"About a week ago and I haven't seen her since. Perhaps when Peter comes, you could both go down and try and talk her round."

I said we would, and we did, but met with no success.

"When the time comes for them to carry me out I promise I won't bite," said our old friend, with one of her rare flashes of humour. "No, I'll go quietly when I'm asked to, that is if the house lets me."

Peter flashed me a sudden look as if to say, 'here we go again', but all he said was, "O.K. I tell you what, Paula and I will organise a protest and we'll march on the town hall and hand our petition asking them to let you stay."

"Don't bother, dear boy," said Mrs Tyack, obviously touched. "Even if they agreed to deviate the road—which they wouldn't—I wouldn't want to live here with that killer right under my nose, but thanks all the same. The only thing I hope and pray is that you and Paula will never travel down it. I'm very afraid you may."

"Does this mean you *will* come to the Farm Cottage?" I said eagerly, "it's very comfortable and warm and gets all the sun."

Mrs Tyack said demurely she would give it her serious consideration. It was more than we had dared to hope for and Peter and I returned home in a state of unjustifiable euphoria.

It didn't last long. Two days later, I was helping mother to make jam when we were electrified to see Polly Trebilcock running up the kitchen garden. She still wore her working apron and her slippers were flapping off her feet.

"Good heavens, whatever is the matter with Polly?" said mother, "I'm afraid something must be wrong at Willow End."

Polly was over the threshold before we could get to the kitchen door and for a moment she couldn't get her breath to speak. Mother signed to me to pour her out some coffee. When I got back to them with the mug, mother was looking puzzled and Polly was crying.

"I can't make head nor tail of what has gone wrong," said mother, "Something about a carpet sweeper and a cat. Now Polly, drink this coffee and then tell us quietly and from the beginning just what has happened."

Polly obeyed and we waited. All the years we had known her we had never seen her lose control like this. The story when we eventually got it certainly had an improbable ring to it. Polly it seemed, had arrived as she always did, at 9 a.m. precisely. She changed as was her custom in the tiny room leading off the kitchen that had once been a large storeroom and then, ready for action, had sallied forth to get Mrs Tyack's breakfast. Not that that took any time at all, consisting as it did of chopped up banana covered with a spoonful of honey and a glass of natural orange juice. When Polly got upstairs she wasn't altogether surprised to find Mrs Tyack's bed neatly made and no sign of her employer. It was not uncommon for Mrs Tyack to decide on an early morning walk when the weather was good and when she did that she invariably made her bed before setting out. Polly, after a brief look round, took the tray downstairs and covering it with a cloth, put it on the kitchen table. Then she set to work.

It actually took a second cup of coffee to bring Polly to the point and even then the point—if indeed there was a point—wasn't altogether as clear as it might have been. Polly decided to start with the sitting room so it would be shipshape when Mrs

Tyack returned. Having no electricity, she had to resort to a carpet sweeper. Jason, Mrs Tyack's black and white cat, was sitting on the window seat watching her. Presently Jason, according to Polly, leapt down from the window seat and began to pace swiftly up and down in short lengths as if he were rubbing himself against somebody's legs, and all the time he was doing it he kept up a shrill purr of apparent excitement. At first Polly, having other things on her mind, didn't take too much notice of the cat's antics but when she reached that part of the carpet occupied by the little creature and gave him a gentle shove with the Ewbank, she declared she saw Jason rise up into the air as if somebody had picked him up. For a brief few seconds Polly stood staring in disbelief at the suspended animal, then panic took over and, dropping the carpet sweeper, she rushed out of the house.

I glanced at mother who avoided my eyes. "Now, Polly," said mother placidly, "Miss Paula and I will walk with you back to Willow End. You will probably find Mrs Tyack there when we get back."

Polly looked rather dubious at this display of optimism on the part of my parent but obediently followed mother, and we accompanied her back to Willow End. The first thing we saw when we got there was Jason washing his face with every appearance of complete indifference. Of Mrs Tyack there was no sign. That afternoon mother rang the police and a search began.

Two days later they found her. The discovery was actually made by two small boys who had been playing in a wood not a mile from Willow End. The boys ran all the way to the police station, arriving very much out of breath. They said they had found a woman's body and she was squashed quite flat. This dramatic description, as it happened, proved to be correct. On examination it was found that every bone in Mrs Tyack's body had been broken. It was as if a huge juggernaut lorry had gone clean over her. As the wood was a good 400 yards from the nearest road, this didn't make any sense at all.

When I heard the news I couldn't help remembering what she had said to Dad at their last meeting. "They can build their road but it will be over my dead body." Was it coincidence, I wondered, or had she had some kind of premonition?

Peter and I were still in our first year at the university when they really began the work on Cornish soil. I remember we both went to the town hall to have a look at the plans and I saw, as Mrs Tyack had forecast, that the line of the road ran straight across the moors and down to Lands End. Another thing too, the wood where our old friend had met her strange death lay straight in the path of the motorway. Our parents talked quite seriously about moving. Neither of them fancied overlooking noisy highways. One day they went up to the Wadebridge area to look at a few houses, two at New Polzeath and another at Rock. The nearest point to the proposed road would then lie seventeen miles away. As I was only due home in the late afternoon, I hadn't accompanied them. After making myself a quick cup of tea, I wandered out to have a look at the extensive devastation of what had once been a peaceful and lovely scene.

It was a calm evening and no clouds marred the blue sky. With the prospect of a free weekend before me I felt at peace with the world. Even the new way presented itself in a more favourable light than it had done hitherto. Change was in the air and when one is young, change is something new and exciting. When you cease to like change it is a sign you have left your youth behind you. I saw myself doing the journey from Exeter to my home in under the hour. Travel was going to be gloriously swift and easy. Gulls wheeled overhead, screaming as if in warning, and listening to them I suddenly remembered Mrs Tyack and the words she had spoken to me only a few days before her death. "I wish I could be certain that you and Peter would never travel on it when it's built, but I am afraid you will." But then Mrs Tyack was old and tired, perhaps at her age people thought in that way! I reached the edge of the great highway still roped off from motor users. On the 27th of the month the Minister of Transport would open this section that went down as far as Fraddon, the flood of traffic would be pouring down it, heading south west. Already hotels and boarding houses had maximum bookings and were jubilant. I even began to regret my parents' decision to move away from it. I stood there looking over the barricades, and then without realising what I was doing, I slipped underneath them and stood on the road itself. The wind blew through my hair and fanned my hot face. I was filled with a sudden excitement and I began to run down the road trying to emulate the speed that was to come. Seen from afar, Mrs Tyack's warnings sounded like the croaking of a raven.

Suddenly, sound exploded all about me. It was as if somebody had opened a door and I found myself staring at a huge juggernaut of a lorry that was charging straight towards me. From where I stood I could feel the reverberation of its thunderous approach on the tarmac; I could almost feel the heat of its vast engines. There was a man sitting in the cab. I could see him and I knew *he could not see me*! I leapt like a frightened animal on to the grass verge and crouched there shaking in every limb. There were other cars, other lorries, overtaking one another, racing faster and faster and in the air I seemed to hear the echo of mad laughter. Then suddenly, as I watched, I saw the first car spinning out of control and after that it was pure nightmare. Nobody seemed able to stop. *No*, I heard myself screaming, *No*, and I turned and ran, head down, away from that horrible vision and stumbled back towards the sane safe world in which I had been brought up.

I knew now how it was Mrs Tyack had met her mysterious death. Was it possible that I had actually seen the monster that had destroyed her? I had recently been reading about 'time warps' but up till that afternoon had put the theory down to the imagination of science fiction writers. After that, however, my ideas on the subject were decidedly less clear cut. One thing I was certain about and that was that whereas I had by some means escaped with my life, my old friend had not.

Then, as suddenly as it had started, the turmoil ceased. It was as if somebody had quietly but firmly closed a heavy door, shutting out all sound. I stopped in my flight and looked back. The half-finished highway was still there in all its hideous confusion but now, instead of the flying traffic, all was quiet. No sounds except the sounds of summer came to my listening ears. Had I fallen asleep on my feet and had a dream?

I walked back to the house hoping I shouldn't meet anybody until I'd got things straightened out in my mind. Jason, who had come to live with us after Mrs Tyack's death, came to meet me, stepping daintily through the long grass, his tail straight up like a poker and his amber eyes gleaming welcome as they always did. I crouched down, glad of the warm loving presence of the little beast. Then, without warning, something else happened. I was aware that Jason had suddenly shifted his gaze. Suddenly, without warning, he had withdrawn from me, his attention was elsewhere. I stood up stiffly and watched him. The little cat ran forwards, then slowly and quite deliberately began to pace up and down within a short area, for all the world as if he was rubbing himself against somebody's legs, and all the time he uttered sharp little cries as if in welcome. I think at that moment I was more frightened than I had been on the highway. I stood there rooted to the spot watching the pacing cat and remembering the morning that mother and I had been making jam and we had seen Polly Trebilcock running up the kitchen garden to recount a strange happening that neither of us believed at the time. Now, it was happening all over again.

It was then that my mind, straining and receptive, found the solution. I thought of that last afternoon when I had visited Mrs Tyack before her death, of something she had said, perhaps it was even the last thing she had said, 'the only thing I hope and pray is that you and Peter will never travel down it but I am afraid you will want to."

Was it possible, I thought, that now, this situation had, in fact, arisen? That Mrs Tyack had somehow or another managed to step in and given me the vision? If so, it was obvious that not only was our old friend quite close but she still cared. Even in my confusion I found that thought very comforting.

Jason stopped pacing and ran up to me. I bent down and took him in my arms. Memories of Mrs Tyack were still crowding in on me, vivid and clear cut. I remembered for instance seeing a fragment of a poem lying on her table. I thought for a moment she had written it herself but she had said with a smile that she had copied it out of a book and now the first two lines came into my mind.

> "Red-rose youth, passionate, pale,
> a singing stream in a silent vale . . ."

It was only then that I realised what a big part Peter and I must have played in her life and I was glad.

Adrian Cole

MIDNIGHT HAG

DALTON HAD BEEN DRIVING ALL NIGHT; the rage still hadn't left him, though its earlier terrible fire had cooled. Why was Beth so difficult? Hadn't he done his best to straighten out the mess of their marriage? He wrenched the steering wheel, badly negotiating a tight bend, veering to the right, but it was okay. Not much traffic about at this time of the morning, especially out here in the country. He yawned, determined to get to Rex's before stopping. Sure, he admitted to himself, he was mainly to blame for the mess, but he'd tried to repair things more than once. She just wouldn't let the past lie, couldn't accept that he'd buried it. His brief affair with Linda had ended long ago; why must Beth insist on a periodic exhumation of that particular corpse?

The car clipped the hedgerow as something shot by on the other side of the road, horn blaring, smothered by the crowding hazel. Rex's place wasn't far, thank God. Dalton could rest once he was there and Rex would be no problem. He'd been a good mate in the past, long before he'd ever retired here to run his country pub. Sensible man. Any time, he'd told Dalton. Well, now was the time. Dalton had needed to get away after last night—far away. Create time to think, to breathe.

This past week had been hellish. Orders pumping in, reps racing around, customers arriving from Germany and Spain, all in need of careful attention, wining and dining. Those orders were essential, damn them. Dalton had felt his head squeezing to bursting point. The late nights had been frantic. Too much bloody booze. Friday had arrived like an iced tonic, and after a long, tedious session with two of his underlings, Dalton's week had been over. Nine o'clock at night. Beth would be waiting, sour-faced and cold.

He had been right; she hadn't approved. He'd grunted a brief explanation, hardly feeling it was worth it, hardly having the energy. He'd needed to relax, not to renew hostilities. Dinner was spoiled—why the hell did she always insist on preparing it when she knew he might be home at any time? Business, he had told her. He was a company dynamo, but the job was running him down. He'd explained about resting, about stopping for a while. It was just impracticable. Once you did that, the axe would fall. They were all after your chair. No rest. In a few years he could pack it in and they could live comfortably off the money he'd made. In a few years.

Beth could have lashed him for his erratic hours—he'd had all that before and had learned to ride it mechanically. He had all the answers in a mental file. But it hadn't been that. She'd been in tears. He'd felt obliged to pry it out of her, wanting to have a quiet weekend. In the end the storm had broken. She had insisted it wasn't his job. She had accused him of having another woman. In the past there had been other women, and he'd given up denying that. But not this time. He was trying, he'd told her. Damn it, he wanted to make it work. This hectic life was too much for him and he was ready to slow down and take things easier. And he needed her to make it easier. But she had refused to listen. He was unreliable, she'd said. How could she believe him, when he'd lied so often before?

On it had gone, rising in pitch to ugliness. I can't stand it, not on top of this grinding week, he'd felt his nerves shout. The row had burst like an abscess, and he'd fled from its flowing poison.

All night he'd driven, heading south and west. Rex would help out. He'd been as wild as Dalton when they were younger, hell-raising together, so he knew all about pressures from home.

The car moved now through the deserted streets of another anonymous village, no more than a few houses, white and sharp in the dawn sunlight. Tyres screeched in pained protestation on the tight bends, needing air. Dalton rubbed at his sore eyes, willing himself on for a little longer. Maybe I should stop . . .

A shadow had detached itself from a lane or turning, moving out into the square at the heart of the tiny hamlet. It danced in the corner of his eye; he swerved, but felt a bump. A bundle of something lurched away towards a wall. Old sacks? But there had been a smear of face—old and raddled. Gone in an instant. The car bit into the road, spinning sideways but halting. Swearing foully, Dalton flung open the door. There were fortunately no onlookers; the village slept. But he had to see whom he had hit, or if they were hurt.

He'd thought it was an old woman, but in the square was nothing. If she'd been hurt, it wasn't badly. Either she'd limped away or managed to get indoors. He looked round. No movement. Didn't seem to be any prying eyes either, though there must be. He looked at the ground for signs of the old woman, but there were no marks in the dusty sandstone soil. The stink of dung assailed his nostrils. A splash of colour caught his eye and he bent down to see a few twisted stems of lavender. He picked them up, sniffing at the fragrance.

No point wasting any more time here. He dropped the lavender and inspected the front bumper of the car. Nothing. If he had hit the silly old mare, it couldn't have been more than a glancing blow. He drove off, relieved to be moving again.

He thought there were going to be problems at first: Rex was in London, ironing out a new financial angle with his bank. However, his wife, Meg, was there to proffer a shoulder.

"Glad to have you with us, Roger! It's about time you looked us up, anyway. Where's Beth?"

Dalton put his overnight bag down beside the bed, looking round the neat room with a nod of satisfaction. "Beth? Let's talk about it later. Right now I need a good sleep, Meg. I'm all in. Been driving all night."

"Oh dear. Row?" she asked, a faint smile pasting itself across her mouth. She leaned against the door jamb, arms folded, head on one side. Attractive, thought Dalton. He'd wondered before now about her. He grunted non-committally.

"Everything all right between you two?"

He took his jacket off and started unbuttoning his shirt. "When I wake up, which will be about four, how about a hot meal?" he grinned.

She nodded. "I'll wake you," she said, managing to inject a hint of something into the words. The door closed softly, almost reluctantly behind her. Dalton rubbed his face, shuffling sleepily into the adjoining bathroom.

He was awake and up before Meg had come to knock at his door. After a thorough wash he changed his shirt and went down in search of the promised meal, which he needed. It was ready and Meg sat opposite him in the bay window of the large kitchen. The window was open, and it remained surprisingly warm.

Dalton ate slowly. "Nice place you've got here. Rex has done well for you. Business good?"

"Good enough," she said with a sigh. "And you? Still running your empire?"

He grunted, thoughts drifting vaguely to Beth.

"And Beth?" She leaned forward, and there was a sharp tang of perfume heavy in the air. It was impossible to ignore her impressive outline.

"Yes, we had a row. Bad one. I took off. I'd had a bastard of a week. I thought coming here would help me think straight."

"You didn't give me a chance to explain earlier—Rex won't be back until next week. Not that it matters."

He pushed his plate away gently. "I see."

"You know, I'm surprised you two have lasted as long as you have. You've no kids either, have you?"

He sipped at the wine Meg had given him. No, no kids, he

thought. Too much of a drawback to his job. "Habit, perhaps."

"Anything else to eat?" she asked, getting up and removing his plate, leaning over him. He demurred, shaking a cigarette from his packet. He offered her one and she took it. "I'll show you around if you like. It's not a bad place. Plenty of grounds."

"Yes, I could do with some fresh air."

She took him over the gardens and showed him the three fields at the back where several horses frisked. In the distance the edge of Dartmoor watched them quietly, mauve in the late afternoon.

"It's certainly beautiful," Dalton nodded. He found it hard to superimpose a picture of the skyline he was familiar with.

Meg leaned on a gate, body arched forward. "It's okay. But I miss the bright lights sometimes. It can get bloody boring. In winter the whole place hibernates."

He studied the line of her body, knowing that her pose was deliberate. "I never did think of you as a country girl, Meg."

She held her position for a moment, then stretched. "I don't know if I am."

They walked back to the buildings and looked over the pub, the plot for the extension.

"You seem to have made a gold mine out of it."

In the private lounge she poured him a drink and sat by him on the deep settee. "Now tell me about you and Beth."

He blew out a cloud of smoke and watched it match the curls of the horse brasses. "You've heard it all before. Tell me about you and Rex."

She laughed. "There's nothing to tell. Absolutely nothing."

Dalton had had a bellyful of businessmen and trendy youngbloods inflated with money. So instead of settling down in the residents' bar that evening, he opted for the locals' bar. Its furnishings were simple, its decor basic, which suited the farmers and villagers who seemed to have little inclination for the brandy and cigars of the other bar (though Dalton had heard that the farmers could well afford the luxuries). They played darts or dominoes, or sat noisily discussing their coming harvest or their livestock.

Dalton was not made to feel like an intruder, for there was nothing introspective about the local inhabitants; they spoke to him and gave him several chances to enter into conversation during the course of the evening. He was also able to do some thinking. His dilemma had worsened, though. He admitted to himself that there was another reason why he had come in here. Meg served the residents, and he wanted to be free of her for a while. She had casually understated her needs, her willingness. Is that what I want? he asked himself more than once. Why should bedding Rex's wife bother him? In the past he had speculated more than once. Guilt, perhaps? Was it, after all, worth trying to patch up his tottering marriage? Part of him wanted to, badly. Perhaps it was something to do with his loathing of failure. Or maybe a groping for stability. Beth had never fought him over having children—was that at the root of her dissatisfaction?

Waiting at the bar, he noticed a calendar pinned up. The naked girl who adorned it smiled provocatively, her golden breasts full, the nipples artificially erect, the hips insolent, inviting. Dalton superimposed Meg's face over the smile, seeing in the lure of the glossy photograph the lust of his friend's wife. But it was only a lust that mirrored his own. He turned away, annoyed with himself.

Meg faced him. "How are you getting on in here?" She swayed over the bar at him. Her presence was becoming a challenge. She drew him for a moment; he sensed a spear of desire. His mouth was unaccountably dry, which was ridiculous—he'd seduced far too many women in the past to be unnerved by Meg, in spite of her obvious approach.

He was about to speak when someone jogged his arm, tapping the counter. Whoever it was was dressed in filthy tatters. They croaked their order impatiently. Dalton snatched his attention from Meg to stare down at the odd creature. He couldn't see the face, but it seemed to be an old man—or was it a woman? A black dress and torn shawl.

"What's the matter?" Meg said, sensing the withdrawal in him. She called the young barman over to deal with the other men who were waiting for fresh pints.

"Who is she?" Dalton blurted under his breath, leaning away from the old woman as though she was diseased.

"What?" said Meg, still smiling.

He tossed back his whisky chaser hurriedly and fumbled for the pint of lager she had pulled for him.

"Why don't you come into the residents' bar, Roger? I'm going to take a breather in a moment. You look too miserable for words!"

He smiled automatically, trying to untie the knot of snakes that writhed in his belly. Abruptly he pushed past the old woman; as he did so, he noticed the sweet smell. Lavender.

Thankfully there were few residents in their bar. He sat on a stool at the counter, glad to be in here. It was suddenly a comfort to talk to Meg, his irrational anxiety negating the undercurrent of meanings in her attitude.

"Are you that worried about Beth?"

He nodded. "She was in a hell of a state. What could I do, though, Meg? I've tried, dammit. I've done everything. But whatever I do, she holds up my past. It's a barrier I can't break. Oh, it's my own damned fault. But I've tried."

She patted his arm gently, her fingers apparently intrigued by his wrist. "You don't have to justify yourself to me. It's no good regretting everything in life. Does she know you're here?"

"Yes. I said I'd go back on Sunday."

"Maybe the break will do you both good." She had sensed his interest sliding from her but remained quietly determined to guide it back. "Look, you'd better call it a night. The booze is never an answer—I know that. I'll fix you some coffee."

He stared at the bedroom ceiling, but its blackness was soiled with images. Beth's shouting mouth, tongue fluttering within it like a trapped animal. It writhed convulsively and became Meg's tongue, reaching out a wet tip for him. Sleep was impossible.

The pub was blessedly silent now. He'd had coffee with Meg, who had sensed his strange moroseness. He didn't understand it himself—it seemed linked to the old woman in the bar. He was sure now that she was the one his car had hit—or thought his car had hit. But she wasn't injured and made no show of having recognised him. He dismissed her for the dozenth time.

Meg had said goodnight without making any further play. He felt instant regret, unsure of his own wants. Now that he was here, uselessly courting sleep, he began to think back over the day—the shape of his hostess and the way she had used it to arouse him, the girl on the calendar, whose sensuous form now wriggled on the ceiling.

He got out of bed, naked, and reached for a cigarette, lighting it at the second attempt. From the tiny window he could look out at the distant moors. He frowned at them, then snorted in vague amusement at their curvaceous outline.

He moved away, glad of an amusing image. The bedroom door was open, its dark mouth filled by a subtle shape. Something soft swished as the form glided to the bed. Fascinated, Dalton saw a pale hand extend to the disturbed bedclothes. It was Meg. She realised he was not there and jerked up stiffly.

"Meg?" he breathed, quickly stubbing out the cigarette.

"You gave me a start," she shivered, moving around the bed.

For some reason it was almost a confrontation. "I couldn't sleep," he began, feeling uneasy.

"There's no need to say anything," she told him. Her face was blotched by the faint streetlight somewhere outside, her form caressed by shadow. He heard the nightdress slip easily to the floor as she climbed on to the bed. He hesitated.

"What's wrong?" she said to his foolish silence.

Slowly he joined her in the darkness, his fingers extending, touching her gently. She shuddered beneath him, breath quickening as he moved over her. He went on touching her for some moments, as if the situation was somehow unreal, and she pulled at him. The urgency of the moment communicated itself to him abruptly and he let it swallow him.

It had ended, as always, in sleep. When he woke it was early morning, a pale light spilling over the sill on to the carpet. He came slowly out of sleep, which had been deep. His arms pushed gently across the bed, seeking out her warm body, the hair tangled by love. His fingers touched her shoulder, but his mind recoiled. Love? Why gloss it? They had been little more than dogs in season. His fingers moved abstractedly. Her skin felt older now, latticed with wrinkles.

In her sleep she wheezed, murmuring as he moved slightly. He looked beyond her to the chair by the bed. On it were clothes he did not recognise. A black dress, and hanging over the chair back, a shawl. Shawl? Whose was that? He stared at it, defying its reality. The mass of hair on the pillow beside him was grey, flecked with red soil. His hand withdrew from the wizened flesh.

He pulled back the sheets and got out of the bed in horror, afraid to look at the sleeping form, still mummified by the remainder of the sheet. Hurriedly he dressed, praying she wouldn't wake. He reached the door, teasing it open.

"Roger?"

It was Meg's voice: he felt her eyes probing him. Controlling himself, he turned. She had sat up in bed, her full breasts dark against the whiteness. Sleepily she patted the bed. "You're an early riser," she yawned. "Come back to bed." She pulled the sheets away to reveal one side of herself. The light was poor, but her form was her own, natural and smooth.

He was tempted to get back into bed. "I . . . want something to drink. A coffee."

"Christ, at this time of the morning?"

"It's an old habit——" he muttered, feeling ridiculous.

She was getting langorously out of bed; he watched her as she slipped her nightdress back on. "I'll make it. You go back to bed. The guests won't be quite so alarmed if they investigate and find me moving about in the kitchen—God, Roger, it's only just turned five-thirty! Do you always get up for a drink——?"

"Yes," he said quickly. "Why not? Look, I'll do it——"

"No, I don't mind." She gave him a slightly puzzled look and a light kiss. "Go back to bed," she added, a note of insistence in her voice. The door closed behind her, condemning him to a possible repetition of the night. But the image of the old woman lingered. It had been real. He spun round, searching for the dress and shawl, but they were gone—if they had ever been there.

He mouthed an obscenity, his fingers reaching for his shirt buttons as he prepared to undress. He stopped. The smell of last night's sex hung heavy, but mingled with something else. Abruptly he wrenched at the door and lurched on to the landing. He was half way down the stairs before he knew what the smell was.

He would leave quietly; just a few words to Meg, an explanation, tell her he'd decided he must go back to Beth and work things out. She'd be angry, but at least he owed Meg some kind of reason. There was no point in abusing her any more.

Beyond the hall the kitchen confronted him, a single source of light in the big house. He could hear her moving around as he edged the door open. "Meg?"

She stood by the cooker, watching the kettle sleepily. His voice tugged her head round. "Aren't you in bed?" she said, as if angry with him.

"No." They both looked embarrassed, recognising the source.

"You're leaving."

"It's best."

"You think a lot more of your wife than I realised." She looked suddenly dejected, tired, her age highlighted in the rude glare of the fluorescent light.

"Well . . . I'll get my bag."

"You'll want something to eat on the way. I'll fix you some sandwiches and a flask. On the house," she added, barely keeping the bitterness from her voice.

He started to speak, but nodded and went back upstairs. When he came down, she had composed herself and gave him a coffee. They sipped together in silence for a while, eyes averted. Meg looked as if she had been wounded, as if his urge to flee was a real disappointment to her. Dalton stared at his coffee, confused by his own emotions.

"Do I make you feel unclean?" she said, pulling her night-dress tighter.

"What?" He'd been distracted. "No . . . don't say that."

"No? I came to you, remember? You could have sent me away. You seemed keen enough last night." She had found her tongue, organising her anger at his abrupt change of feeling.

"Yes I know," he agreed, still evading the stare. "I know. I didn't know what I wanted."

She thought better of arguing. "I just can't believe you're so concerned about it. You, of all people."

He pushed his cup away as if it irked him. What the hell did she want from him? "I'm sorry, that's all. I want to go back."

She nodded, hands shaking, holding her cup tightly to steady them. "Yes, I'm sorry, too. I know how you feel. Hell, that's bloody corny. But I do know. Rex and I are a habit, to use your own word. A bloody habit."

He looked at her, seeing the pained frustration in her eyes, the years wasted in resentment. His hand reached over the table dividing them and touched her fingers. "It isn't you."

She waited, expecting him to explain something, but he

couldn't put words to his absurd phobia about the old woman. Instead he rose, picking up his bag. "I'll get back home. It's a long drive."

Together they went into the hall, where the shadows were absorbed by the carpet as the day took hold.

"Come down again some time," she said, facing him.

"I will," he lied. Her mouth waited, the lips parting in a last attempt to draw him back. He bent to her, meaning to kiss her lightly, but her lips fastened on to his, her tongue thrusting into his mouth. She gripped him, grinding her body against him. He forced his mouth away, startled by her desperation.

"You can still change your mind," she said with surprising vehemence. "Why the hell must you rush off so early? Stay a while, Roger—please." Her hands pulled his over her flesh, pushing them down on her breasts.

There were eyes watching—hateful eyes, he was certain. He looked down the hall to the outside door. It had opened, silhouetting the figure of a woman against the blue of daylight.

"*Beth!*" he cried, choking on the name. But the door slammed shut at once as the figure withdrew.

"What?" said Meg, flushed.

"She's followed me!" He broke away and ran down the hall.

"Wait!" Meg protested, hastily reaching for a coat, but he ignored her. The front door shut behind him, crushing the last of her hopes. She bit back the tears, the sense of betrayal.

Dalton was outside, appalled by the arrival of his wife. How much had she seen? Christ, Meg had been virtually naked, and his hands had been all over her. Beth would never listen to reason now. She'd know it all, piece together the whole sordid night.

"Beth!"

There were a few cars in the car park; he looked at them briefly. At the far end he saw her car and beside it a flurry of movement. The car door thumped shut in disgust. "Wait!" he shouted. In his frenzy he misjudged the granite steps and sprawled. As he got up he heard the car roar by angrily. By the time he had recovered, she had driven on to the road and was disappearing. He fumbled with his own car keys, starting up and revving the engine, determined to stop her and explain. But what was there to explain? There were no excuses. He had told her he was leaving her because she was unreasonable, accusing him of womanising, and she'd followed him, possibly to apologise, only to catch him in the very act. The car tore out of the car park and he gave only a brief thought to Meg. He could never go back.

He stamped the accelerator and the car bounced forward, giving chase. If he couldn't stop her now, the marriage was certainly over.

He could see Beth's car some distance ahead of him, flashing in the sunlight up one of the winding gradients. The dip and swell of the landscape alternately swallowed and disgorged her as she sped on. If she reached the distant motorway before he caught her up, he doubted he would catch her: she could drive like a maniac when she had a mind to.

An oncoming horn blared at Dalton, a banshee of scorn for his erratic driving. He fixed his eyes on the road ahead, determined to bring Beth's car within reach. The land was rising, signposts flashing by in an unreadable blur. This was not the way he had come south. Not the way home. Beth must be driving anywhere, her resentment and anger aiming her nowhere in particular. Like her temper, her car took the most accessible outlet.

The moors loomed above the fields and the two cars clanged over an old cattle grid, now separated by no more than a hundred yards. Dalton wore a fixed grin as he trod the accelerator hard again. He was gaining. He would best her yet. He always wore her down—she always submitted. Failure was unthinkable. The rush of adrenalin made him careless, but the road was open and empty. No one would slow him. Beth would never shake him.

Finally, tacky with sweat, he pulled level with her. Hair obscured her face and she ignored him as he shouted at her to pull over. For half a mile they raced alongside, Dalton anxiously trying to make her stop and give in. There was a sudden dip in the road and a bridge sped at them. Tyres bit into macadam, stones flew up like angry insects. At last Beth had braked, rather than slam into stonework.

Dalton edged the nose of his car beyond hers as he braked. The two vehicles skidded to a halt at the grass verge, wheels thudding into a drainage ditch. Dalton smacked his head against the dashboard and swore at the immediate ooze of blood. But he was okay. He wrestled the door open and sucked in a lungful of air. He turned to his wife's car, but the side door leaned at an angle. She had left it. His eyes roamed the moor and saw her figure not far off, running up the shallow valley of a riverbed that had almost dried up in the heat. But she wouldn't get away from him now.

He shouted, taking up the pursuit, aware now of his passions, strangely aroused by the situation. Beth had become more than a fleeing figure to be caught. She was the object of a burning desire. He must reach her. He must take her. She couldn't evade him. She must see reason. If not, he would *take* her. She was his wife. There was no law that would protect her.

He raced over the granite boulders, heedless of the danger; a fall here could result in a broken leg easily, but his emotions were in a turmoil, blotting out everything but his desire. Last night's images laughed at him. He could feel Meg's urgent flesh.

Beth was only yards ahead. He could hear sobs as she dragged in laboured breaths. "Wait!" he shouted, but she refused to listen. There were a few gnarled trees here, stunted oaks bent double by the prevailing winds. In the shade of them she stumbled. His hands reached out roughly and gripped her shoulders.

"Beth," he breathed thickly, leaning over her in a kind of mad triumph. She looked up at him, her face smeared with tears, her head shaking.

"Beth," he repeated, breath a hot rasp in his throat. "I'm sorry . . ." he blurted, words useless here. She saw the turmoil in him and cowered back among the sparse ferns.

"No, Roger, please."

"Beth," he murmured again, dropping beside her. He began pulling at her clothes. She shrieked, but it was pointless in so secluded a valley, out of sight of the road. She shook her head, making only a token effort to stop him as he tore her blouse from her and attacked her skirt. He bruised her carelessly as he exposed her. She thrashed as he forced himself on her, his head ringing, heart thunder within him.

Her cries became a whimper that trailed off into silence. The madness of the act washed over him in a sticky tide, its waves receding slowly until he was aware of the cool morning breeze, his passion spent. He drew his mouth from her hair and stared into her face. It was devoid of expression. He had never really made her respond, now or in all their years together. For her, he was impotent.

She said nothing, registered no emotion. Carefully, remorsefully, he did what he could to dress her. When he had finished, he helped her to her feet. She still said nothing, dummy-like, making no attempt to walk. He swung her up into his arms and began the laboured journey down the gully to the cars.

Exhausted, he put her in the back seat of his own car. He'd have a garage come out and pick hers up later. Wiping his face down with his handkerchief, he stared at his haggard face in the mirror. Christ, what a mess! What had he done! What had possessed him to act like an animal? He glanced at Beth, but she was mercifully asleep, like a child. She almost looked comfortable.

The drive back over the moors made him uneasy; he kept reliving the rape. He'd never felt the need for her so strongly before. He could not have stopped himself. But . . . had he ever done less than rape her? Again he looked in the mirror, but she remained asleep.

As these unpleasant reflections harried him, he tried to find an escape in the radio. Music gushed around the car and he twisted the dial in annoyance. An alternative channel offered him a news bulletin.

> '. . . a spokesman said later that everything was being done to keep the price down, although a rise is certain in the next few months.
>
> Police are still searching for Roger Dalton, the Leicestershire businessman, who has been missing since last night. They are anxious to locate Dalton with regard to his wife's suicide last night in their Leicester home. Mrs Elizabeth Dalton was found early this morning. She had taken an overdose of sleeping pills and died during the night . . .'

He stared in horror at the radio, as if he would see the bland face of the newscaster. The remainder of the broadcast was lost in a murmur as Dalton felt his mind veering. There was a movement behind him. He fought the urge to look in the mirror. Something touched his shoulder. The stuffy interior of the car was permeated with the overpowering, sweet smell of lavender.

Elizabeth Fancett

BABY HATE

GARY WAS CONVINCED THAT HIS BABY son, Paul, hated him. From the very first moment that Helen had brought him home from the hospital the child would scream and yell with rage every time that Gary attempted to go near him, and whenever Gary kissed his wife in the presence of Paul there were sure to be the same screams, the same show of rage. And one evening, when Gary had tried to give Paul his bottle, the enraged infant struck it from his grasp with a tiny clenched fist and sent it shattering to the floor.

"He hates me." Gary told his wife gloomily. "That's quite obvious. He hates the very sight of me."

"Nonsense!" said Helen, smiling. "How can such a small baby possibly hate? It hasn't yet developed any such emotions."

"This one has," said Gary grimly. "And this one hates me. From now on, I don't intend to go anywhere near him. We don't want the neighbours to think we're bashing him, do we?"

For a long while, Gary managed to keep out of Paul's way—even out of his sight, whenever possible. For, if ever he came into the child's range of vision, the baby would go into terrible fits of screaming rage.

But the abnormal situation began telling on them both. Helen was becoming thin and ill with the strain of having to cope with Paul single-handed, coupled with the constant anxiety of trying to keep him out of Gary's way. Gary was becoming more and more upset and morose by the baby's hostile attitude towards him. At last Helen could stand things no longer and she decided to secretly consult a psychiatrist about the bizarre situation.

"It is extremely unlikely," the psychiatrist told her gravely, "that a small baby should possess such strong feelings and emotions—especially one of hatred, which is the most powerful of all the emotions."

"Then what *is* wrong with him?" demanded Helen. "My husband dare not even let the baby *see* him, let alone go near him! I'm exhausted trying to cope alone with him and at the same time keep him out of Gary's way."

"Have you considered," said the psychiatrist thoughtfully "—now you're not going to like this suggestion but I feel it has to be made—have you considered that it might be the other way about?"

"What do you mean—the other way about?" asked Helen.

"Perhaps," said the psychiatrist, "it is your *husband* who hates the *baby*—and the child's fits of apparent rage could, instead, be fear. Fear is an instinct of which we are all capable from the very early hours of birth until death."

Helen was deeply shocked. She hadn't even considered that possibility.

"It is far more likely," went on the psychiatrist, "than the possibility that the child is capable of hating his father."

"No!" said Helen, angry now. "Gary loves Paul! You've no idea how upset he is because of the child's attitude towards him. Gary wouldn't hate *anyone*—least of all his own son!"

"Not consciously, perhaps," agreed the psychiatrist. "It could be that he is even fighting the emotion—which is linked to a natural jealousy—but subconsciously, deep down inside him, the feeling of hate may persist. And it could be that the baby senses this."

He was serious, Helen could see that, and the idea distressed her even more than her child's apparent aversion to her husband. The implication of what it might mean—if it were true—flooded over her. Supposing, she thought, just supposing that Gary did subconsciously hate his son. Might there not come a time when circumstances would force her to leave Paul alone with him? And if the child screamed . . . and Gary lost his temper, realising the hate welling up in him . . . The finished thought was too terrible to contemplate. She shuddered, fighting the awful picture conjured up in her mind. One thing was certain in the light of this possibility—and she was forced to admit that it was plausible—she could never leave Paul alone with Gary. Never.

Gary was growing more and more concerned about his wife, a concern that overrode even the constant distress caused him by his relationship with his own son. Helen looked so pale, so exhausted. She was with the child all the time, took him everywhere with her, and at night when Paul woke, crying, it was always she who must attend to him. Helen was, he thought, heading fast for a breakdown.

"Look, love," he said one Saturday, "you can't go on like this. Can't you leave Paul at home just this once? You must have a break—or you'll have a break*down*! Go and buy those clothes you need. I promise I won't even go near Paul. He's asleep now, anyway, and he can wait for his feed until you come back, can't he?"

Helen was sorely tempted. It might work, mightn't it? If Paul didn't see Gary then Paul wouldn't scream, and if Paul didn't scream there would be no need for Gary . . . She cut off her thoughts sharply. It was monstrous of her to think that Gary would hurt such a tiny baby—especially *their* baby! It was monstrous of her to think that Gary could hate Paul even subconsciously. He was so obviously upset, wasn't he, by the baby's attitude towards him? No, the psychiatrist must have been wrong and she should never have gone to him in the first place. Thank God Gary didn't know of her visit.

"All right," she agreed. "I won't be long though, and I'll make up his feed before I go so that he can have it straight away when I come home. With any luck, he'll sleep right through while I'm gone."

"Take your time, love," said Gary. "If he does happen to

wake because he's hungry—well, he may cry for a while perhaps but he won't scream blue murder, which he would do if I went in to him and tried to give him his bottle."

Helen spent a happy hour trying on clothes before she began to grow anxious again. She wondered how Gary was coping. Had Paul woken up? Was his crying distressing Gary? Perhaps if she rang up home, just to make sure . . .? She could stay a little longer then, if everything was all right.

She went to the shop telephone kiosk and dialled her number. There was a slight pause before she heard the receiver lifted the other end.

Then "Hello," said Gary. To her intense relief, his voice sounded cheerful, normal.

"Everything's all right then?" she said happily.

"Sure, darling, everything's okay. Not a sound from Paul so far, he's——"

Gary's voice broke off. Faintly, in the background, from the half-open door of his room, she heard Paul's cry.

"The phone must have woken him!" said Gary quickly. "And now he's heard my voice!"

She could hear Paul starting to scream now.

Gary's voice was agitated, scared. "I'll have to do something, honey! I'll have to do something!"

"No!" she screamed. "Don't go near him! Don't you touch him!"

But Gary didn't answer. She guessed he had dropped the receiver and had gone into Paul's room. Nothing sounded in her ears now but the awful, terrified, almost maniacal screaming. Presently, she heard a terrible shout above the screaming. Then nothing. Silence. She stood petrified, listening, her mind a confusion of wild, chaotic thoughts. Should she phone the local police . . . ask them to go there and save her baby? But how could she do that to Gary—he was her husband! And what if she were wrong? No, she must get there herself—and quickly!

Without even replacing the receiver, she ran out of the shop and into the street. There was no time to wait for a bus . . . she must get home. She ran fast, feet flying, heart pounding, her mind racing with terror of what she might find when she reached home, of what might be happening at this very moment. Faster and faster along the pavement she sped, pushing people roughly aside as faster and faster she ran. Get home, get home: Oh, God, let her get home!

The bungalow was in sight now and soon she was racing up the front path. She fumbled in her handbag for the keys, opened the door and stumbled inside.

The place was silent. Very still. With dread, she entered the living room. Paul's bedroom door was open. Trembling, she approached it and looked in. From where she stood she could just see the wooden cot. She came further inside.

The scream that rose from her throat seemed almost to shatter her body and rip her skull apart. The bright clean baby bedclothes were spattered with blood and splintered glass and spilt milk. On the floor by the broken feeding bottle, in a pool of blood and spilt milk, his features hideous and unrecognisable from the jagged glass that had been driven savagely into his face—lay Gary.

And in the cot, amid the blood and the milk and the broken-off neck of the feeding bottle, lay Paul, peacefully sleeping, a small blissful smile of triumph on his tiny face.

Robert Aickman

THE FETCH

IN ALL THAT MATTERS, I WAS an only child. There was a brother once, but I never saw him, even though he lived for several years. My father, a Scottish solicitor or law agent, and very much a Scot, applied himself early to becoming an English barrister, and, as happens to Scots, was made a Judge of the High Court when barely in middle age.

In Court, he was stupendous. From the first, I was taken once every ten days by Cuddy, my nurse, to the public gallery in order to behold him and hearken to him for forty minutes or so. If I made the slightest stir or whimper, it was subtly but effectively repaid me, on those and all other occasions. Judges today are neither better nor worse than my father, but they are different.

At home, my father, only briefly visible, was as a wraith with a will and power that no-one available could resist. The will and power lingered undiminished when my father was not in the house, which, in the nature of things, was for most of the time. As well as the Court and the chambers, there were the club and the dining club, the livery company and the military historical society, all of which my father attended with dedication and sacrifice. With equal regularity, he pursued the cult of self-defence in several different branches, and with little heed for the years. He was an elder of a Scottish church in a London suburb, at some distance from where we lived. He presided over several successive Royal Commissions, until one day he threw up his current presidency in a rage of principle, and was never invited again. After his death, I realised that a further centre of his interest had been a club of a different kind, a very expensive and sophisticated one. I need not say how untrue it is that Scots are penny-scraping in all things.

I was terrified of my father. I feared almost everything, but there was nothing I feared more than to encounter my father or to pick up threads from his intermittent murmurings in the corridors and closets. We lived in a huge house at the centre of Belgravia. No judge could afford such an establishment now. In addition, there was the family home of Pollaporra; modest, comfortless and very remote. Our ancestry was merely legal and commercial, though those words have vastly more power in Scotland than in England. In Scotland, accomplishments are preferred to graces. As a child, I was never taken to Pollaporra. I never went there at all until much later, on two occasions, as I shall unfold.

I was frightened also of Cuddy, properly Miss Hester MacFerrier, and not least when she rambled on, as Scottish women do, of the immense bags and catches ingathered at Pollaporra by our ancestors and their like-minded acquaintances. She often emphasised how cold the house was at all times and how far from a "made road". Only the elect could abide there, one gathered; but there were some who could never bear to leave, and who actually shed tears upon being compelled by the advancing winter to do so. When the snow was on the ground, the house could not be visited at all; not even by the factor to the estate, who lived down by the sea loch, and whose name was Mason. Cuddy had her own methods for compelling the attention of any child to every detail she cared to impart. I cannot recall when I did not know about Mason. He was precisely the man for a Scottish nursemaid to uphold as an example.

My father was understood to dislike criminal cases, which, as an advanced legal theorist and technician, he regarded with contempt. He varied the taking of notes at these times by himself sketching in lightning caricature the figures in the dock to his left. The caricatures were ultimately framed, thirty or forty at a time; whereafter Haverstone, the odd-job man, spent upwards of a week hanging them at different places in our house, according to precise directions written out by my father, well in advance. Anybody who could read at all, could at any time read every word my father wrote, despite the millions of words he had to set down as a duty. Most of the other pictures in our house were engravings after Landseer and Millais and Paton. Generations of Scottish aunts and uncles had also contributed art works of their own, painstaking and gloomy.

I was afraid of Haverstone, because of his disfigurements and his huge size. I used to tiptoe away whenever I heard his breathing. I never cared or dared to ask how he had come to be so marked. Perhaps my idea of his bulk was a familiar illusion of childhood. We shall scarcely know—in that Haverstone, one day after my seventh birthday, fell from a railway bridge into the main road beneath and was destroyed by a lorry. Cuddy regarded Haverstone with contempt, and never failed to claim that my father employed him only out of pity. I never knew what he was doing on the railway bridge, but later I became aware of a huge mental hospital nearby and drew obvious conclusions.

My mother I adored and revered. For better or for worse, one knows the words of Stendhal: "My mother was a charming woman, and I was in love with my mother . . . I wanted to cover my mother with kisses and wished there weren't any clothes . . . She too loved me passionately. She kissed me, and I returned those kisses sometimes with such passion that she had to leave me." Thus it was with me; and, as with Stendhal, so was the sequel.

My mother was very dark, darker than me, and very exotic. I must suppose that only the frenzy of Scottish lust brought my father to marrying her. At such times, some Scots lose hold on all other considerations; in a way never noticed by me among Englishmen. By now, my father's fit was long over. At least he did not intrude upon us, as Stendhal's father did. I am sure that jealousy was very prominent in my father, but perhaps he scorned to show it. He simply kept away from his wife entirely. At least as far as I could see. And I saw most things, though facing far from all of them, and acknowledging none of them.

Day after day, night after night, I lay for hours at a time in my mother's big bed, with my head between her breasts, and my tongue gently extended, as in infancy. The room was perfumed, the bed was perfumed, her nightdress was perfumed, she was perfumed. To a child, it set the idea of Heaven. Who wants any other? My mother's body, as well as being so dark, was softer all over than anyone else's, and sweeter than anything merely physical and fleeting, different and higher altogether. Her rich dark hair, perfumed of itself, fell all about me, as in the East.

There was no social life in our home; no visiting acquaintances, no family connections, no chatter. My father had detached himself from his own folk by his marriage. My mother loved no-one but me. I am sure of that. I was in a position to know. The only callers were her hairdresser, her dressmaker, her maker of shoes and boots, her parfumier, her fabricator of lingerie, and perhaps one or two others of the kind. While she was shorn, scented and fitted, I sat silently in the corner on a little grey hassock. None of the callers seemed to object. They knew the world and what it was like, and would soon enough be like for me. They contained themselves.

I was there whatever my mother did; without exception.

Cuddy dragged me off at intervals for fresh air, but not for very long. I could see for myself that Cuddy, almost familiar with my father, was afraid of my mother. I never knew why, and am far from certain now, but was glad of the fact. It was the key circumstance that transformed the potential of utter wretchedness for me into utter temporary bliss.

My mother taught me all I know that matters—smiling and laughing and holding me and rewarding me, so that always I was precocity incarnate: alike in concepts, dignity and languages. Unfortunately, my mother was often ill, commonly for days, sometimes for weeks, and who was there to care, apart from me, who could do nothing—even if there was something that others could have done? My lessons ceased for a spell, but as soon as possible, or sooner, were bravely resumed.

Later, I strayed through other places of education, defending myself as best I could, and not unsuccessfully either; and, of what I needed, learning what I could. It was not my father who despatched me. He regarded me without interest or expectation. To him I was the enduring reminder of a season's weakness. The ultimate care of me lay with Trustees, as often in Scotland, though only once did I see them as individuals, and hardly even then, because the afternoon was overcast, and all the lights were weak, for some reason that I forget.

Before all that formal education, I had encountered the woman on the stairs. This brief and almost illusory episode was the first of the two turning points in my life and I suspect the more important.

I had been playing on the landing outside the door of my mother's room. I do not know how long she had been ill that time. I feared to count the days, and never did so. I am not sure that it was longer than on various previous occasions. I was alarmed, as always, but not especially alarmed.

My mother had been instrumental in my being given a railway, a conjuring outfit and a chemical set: those being the things that small boys were supposed to like. My father should have given me soldiers, forts and guns; possibly a miniature, but accurate, cricket bat: but he never once gave me anything, or spoke at all in our house if he could avoid it—except, on unpredictable occasions, to himself, memorably, as I have hinted.

I mastered the simple illusions, and liked the outfit, but had no-one to awe. Even my mother preferred to hug me than for me to draw the ace of spades or a tiny white rabbit from her soft mouth. The chemical effects, chlorine gas and liquid air, I never mastered at that time, nor wished to. The railway I loved (no other word), though it was very miniature: neither 1 gauge (in those days) nor O gauge, but something smaller than OO. The single train, in the Royal Bavarian livery of before the First World War, clinked round a true circle; but en route it traversed a tunnel with two cows painted on top and one painted sheep, and passed through two separate stations, where both passengers and staff were painted on the tin walls, and all the signs were in Gothic.

That day, I had stopped playing, owing to the beating of my heart, but I had managed to pack everything into the boxes. I needed no bidding to do that, and never had done. I was about to lug the heap upstairs, which by then I could perfectly well do. I heard the huge clock in the hall strike half-past three. The clock had come from Pollaporra, and reached to the ceiling. I looked at my watch, as I heard it. I was always doing that. It was very late autumn, just before Christmas, but not yet officially winter. There is nothing in this world I know better than exactly what day of the year it was. It is for ever written in the air before me.

My ears were made keen by always listening. Often, wherever I was, even at the top of the house, I waited motionless for the enormous clock to strike, lest the boom take me by surprise. But the ascending woman was upon me before I had heard a footfall. I admit that all the carpets were thickest Brussels and Wilton. I often heard footfalls, none the less, especially my father's strangely uneven tread. I do not think I heard the woman make a sound from first to last. But last was very close to first.

She had come up the stairs beyond doubt, even though I had neither heard nor seen anything, because by the time I did observe her, she was still two or three steps from the top of the flight. It was a wide staircase, but she was ascending in a very curious way, far further from the rail than was necessary and far nearer to the wall, and with her head and face actually turned to the wall.

At that point, I did hear something. I heard someone shut the front door below, which could not be seen from where I stood. I was surprised that I had not heard the door being opened, and the words of enquiry and caution. I remember my surprise. All these sounds were unusual in our house at that time.

I felt the cold air that the woman had brought in with her from the December streets and squares, and a certain cold smell; but she never once turned towards me. She could easily have been quite unaware of me; but I was watching her every motion. She had black hair, thin and lank. She was dressed in a dirty red and blue plaid of some kind, tightly wound. I was of course used to pictures of people in plaids. The woman's shoes were cracked and very unsuited to the slush outside. She moved with short steps, and across the carpet she left a thin trail of damp, though I knew that it was not raining. It was one of the things I always knew. Everything about the woman was of a kind that children particularly fear and dislike. Women, when frightening, are to children enormously more frightening than any man or men.

I think I was too frightened even to shrink back. As the woman tottered past, I stood there with my boxes beside me. My idea of her motion was that she had some difficulty with it, but was sustained by extreme need. Perhaps that is a fancy that only came to me later.

I never had any doubt about where the woman was going but, even so, I was unable to move or to speak or to do anything at all.

As she traversed the few yards of the landing, she extended her right arm and grimy hand from out of her plaid, the hand and arm nearer to me, still without in any degree turning her head. In no time at all, and apparently without looking, she had opened the door of my sweet mother's room, had passed within and had shut the door behind her.

I suppose it is unnecessary for me to say that when my mother was ill, her door was never locked; but perhaps it is not unnecessary. I myself never entered at such times. My mother could not bear me to see her when she was ill.

There was no-one sympathetic to whom I could run crying and screaming. In such matters, children are much influenced by the facilities available. For me, there was only my mother, and, in fact, I think I might actually have gone in after the woman, though not boldly. However, before I was able to move at all, I heard Cuddy's familiar clump ascending the stair behind me as I gazed at the shut door.

"What are you doing now?" asked Cuddy.

"Who was that?" I asked.

"Who was who?" Cuddy asked me back. "Or what?"

"The woman who's gone in there."

"Whist! It's time *you* were in bed with Christmas so near."

"It *wasn't* Father Christmas," I cried.

"I daresay not," said Cuddy. "Because it wasn't anybody."

"It was, Cuddy. It *was*. Go in and look."

It seems to me that Cuddy paused at that for a moment, though it may only have been my own heart that paused.

It made no difference.

"It's bed for you, man," said Cuddy. "You're over-excited and we all know where that ends."

Needless to say, it was impossible for me to sleep, either in the dark or in the light—the choice being always left to me, which was perhaps unusual in those days. I heard the hours and the half-hours all through the night, and at one or two o'clock my father's irregular step, always as if he were dodging something or someone imperfectly seen, and his periodical mutterings and jabberings as he plodded.

All was deeply upsetting to a child, but I must acknowledge that by then I was reasonably accustomed to most of it. One explanation was that I had no comparisons available. As far as I knew, all people behaved as did those in my house. It is my adult opinion that many more, in fact, do so behave than is commonly supposed, or at least acknowledged.

Still, that night must have proved exceptional for me, because when Cuddy came to call me in the morning, she found that I was ill too. Children, like adults, have diseases that it is absurd to categorise. Most diseases, perhaps all, are mainly a collapse or part-collapse of the personality. I daresay a name for that particular malady of mine might in those days have been brain fever. I am not sure that brain fever is any longer permitted to be possible. I am sure that my particular malady went on for weeks, and that when I was once more deemed able to make sense out of things, I learned that my mother was dead, and, indeed, long buried. No-one would tell me where. I further gathered that there was no memorial.

About four weeks after that, or so it now seems to me, but perhaps it was longer, I was told that my father was proposing to remarry, though he required the consent of the Trustees. A judge was but a man as far as the Trustees were concerned, a man within the scope of their own settlement and appointment. Thus it was that I acquired my stepmother; née Miss Agnes Emily Fraser, but at the moment a widow, Mrs Johnny Robertson of Baulk. To her the Trustees had no objection, it seemed.

I still have no idea of why my father married Agnes Robertson, or why he remarried at all. I do not think it can have been the motive that prompted his earlier marriage. From all that, since his death, I have learned of his ways, the notion would seem absurd. It was true that the lady had wealth. In the end, the Trustees admitted as much, and that much of it was in Burmah Oil. I doubt whether this was the answer either. I do not think that more money could have helped my father very much. I am not sure that by then anything could have helped him. This is confirmed by what happened to him, conventional in some ways though it was.

Moreover, the marriage seemed to me to make no difference to his daily way of life: the bench, the chambers, the club, the dining club, the livery company, the military historical society, the self-defence classes, the kirk—or, I am sure, to those other indulgences. On most nights, he continued to ponder and by fits and starts to cry out. I still tiptoed swiftly away and, if possible, hid myself when I heard his step. I seldom set eyes upon my stepmother, though of course I am not saying that I never did. I took it for granted that her attitude to me was at least one thing that she shared with my father. That seemed natural. I found it hard to see what else she had any opportunity of sharing. It had, of course, always been Cuddy to whom I was mainly obliged for information about my father's habits and movements, in so far as she knew them. Cuddy was much less informative about my stepmother.

One new aspect of my own life was that my lessons had stopped. I believe that for more than a year I had nothing to do but keep out of the way and play, as far as was possible. Now there seemed to be no callers at all, and assuredly not parfumiers and designers of lingerie. No doubt my stepmother's circle was entirely in Scotland, and probably to the north of the Forth and Clyde Canal. She would not have found it easy to create an entirely new circle in Belgravia. I suppose there were two reasons why I suffered less than I might have done from the unsatisfactory aspects of my situation. The first was that I could hardly suffer more than I was suffering from my sweet mother's death. The second reason was my suspicion that any other life I might be embarked upon would be even more unsatisfactory.

In the end, the Trustees intervened, as I have said; but before that, Cuddy had something to impart—at long last—about my stepmother. She told me that my stepmother was drinking.

It debarred her, Cuddy informed me in a burst of gossip, from appearing in public very often. That was exactly how Cuddy expressed it; with a twinkle or a glint or whatever may be the Scottish word for such extra intimations. I gathered that my stepmother seldom even dressed herself, or permitted herself to be dressed by Cuddy. One thing I was not told and do not positively know is whether or not the poor lady was drinking as hard as this before her second marriage. It is fair to her to say that the late Johnny Robertson was usually described as a scamp or rogue. Certainly my stepmother's current condition was something that would have had to be concealed by everyone as far as possible at that time in Belgravia, and with her husband a High Court Judge.

In any case, after the Trustees had taken me away and sent me to an eminent school, I began to hear tales. At first, I knocked about those who hurled and spat them at me. I discovered a new strength in the process; just as the grounding (to use the favoured word) provided by my mother, enabled me to do better than most in class, not so much by knowing more as by using greater imagination and ingenuity—qualities that tell even in rivalry among schoolboys. The jibes and jeers ceased, and then I began cautiously to enquire after the facts. The school was of the kind attended by many who really know such things. I learned that my father too had long been drinking, and was a byword for it in the counties and the clubs. No doubt in the gaols also, despite my father's dislike of criminal jurisdiction.

One morning, Jesperson, who was the son of a Labour ex-minister and quite a friend of mine, brought me *The Times* so that I could see the news before others did. I read that my father had had to be removed from his Court and sent for treatment. *The Times* seemed to think that if the treatment were not successful, he might feel it proper to retire. There was a summary of the cases over which he had presided from such an unusually early age (some of them had been attended by me, however fleetingly), and a reference to his almost universal popularity in mainly male society.

I was by then in a position at school to take out any chagrin I might feel upon as many other boys as I wished, but I was too introspective for any such easy release, and instead began for the first time to read the Divine Comedy.

There was nothing particularly unusual in what had happened to my father so far but the treatment seems, as far as one can tell, to have been the conclusive ordeal, so that he died a year later in a mental hospital, like poor Haverstone, though not in the same one. My father returned in spirit to his sodden, picturesque wilderness, and is buried in the kirkyard four or five miles by a very rough road from Pollaporra. It was the first instruction in his Will, which the Trustees heeded, as a matter of urgency, to the last detail.

I could not myself attend the funeral, as I was laid low by a school epidemic, though by then in my last term and older than any of my confrères. My stepmother also missed the funeral, though she had returned to Scotland as soon as she could. She had resolved to remain there and, for all I know, she is there still, with health and sobriety renewed. Several times I have looked her up in directories and failed to find her, despite reference to all three of her known surnames; but I reflect that she may well have married yet again.

My father had left her a moiety of his free estate, in equal part with the various organisations he wished to benefit, and which I have already listed. She possessed, as I have said, means of her own. My father left me nothing at all but he lacked power, Judge though he was and a Scots solicitor also, to modify the family settlement. Therefore I, as only surviving child, inherited a life-interest in Pollaporra, though not in the house in Belgravia, and a moderate, though not remarkable, income for life. Had my brother survived, he would have inherited equally. Thinking about him, I wondered whether the demon drink, albeit so mighty among Scotsmen, had not rather been a symptom of my father's malady than the cause of it. Thinking of that, I naturally then thought about my own inwardness and prospects. Eugene O'Neill says that we become like our parents of the same sex, even when we consciously resolve not to. I wept for my mother, so beloved, so incomparable.

II

Immediately, the question arose of my going to a university. The idea had of course been discussed before with the Trustees, but I had myself rejected it. While my father had been alive, my plan had been simply to leave the country as soon as I could. Thanks to my mother, I had made a good start with two European languages, and I had since advanced a little by reading literature written in them: "Die Räuber" and "Gerusalemme Liberata". The other boys no longer attacked or bullied me when they found me doing such things, and the school library contained a few basic texts, mostly unopened, both in the trade and the literal sense.

Now I changed my mind. The Trustees were clamant for Edinburgh, as could be expected, but I scored an important victory in actually going to Oxford. Boys from that school did not proceed to Edinburgh University, or did not then. It had never been practicable to send me to Fettes or Loretto. My friend Jesperson was at Oxford already. Oxford was still regarded by many as a dream, even though mainly in secret and in silence.

I read modern languages and modern history and I graduated reasonably, though not excitingly. I surprised myself by making a number of friends. This brought important benefits, in the short term and the long.

I now had no home other than Pollaporra which, as will be recalled, could not always be visited during the winter in any case. I spent most of the vacations with new friends—staying in their homes for astonishingly generous periods of time, or travelling with them, or reading with them. With the Second World War so plainly imminent and so probably apocalyptic, everyone travelled as much as he could. I met girls, and was continually amazed by myself. My closest involvement was with a pretty girl who lived in the town who wrote poetry that was published, and who was almost a cripple. That surprised me most of all. I had learned something about myself, though I was unsure what it was. The girl lived, regardless, at the top of the house, which taught me something further. Her name was Celia. I fear that I brought little happiness to her or to any of the others, do what I would. I soon realised that I was a haunted man.

As for the main longer term benefit, it was simple enough, and a matter of seemingly pure chance. My friend, Jack Oliver, spoke to his uncle and as soon as I went down, modestly though not gloriously endorsed, I found myself en route to becoming a merchant banker. I owe Jack a debt that nothing can repay. That too is somehow a property of life. Nothing interlocks or properly relates. Life gives, quite casually with one hand, and takes away rather more with the other hand, equally unforeseeably. There is little anyone can do about either transaction. Jack Oliver was and is the kindest man I have known, and a splendid offhand tennis player. He has a subtle wit, based on meiosis. From time to time he has needed it. I have never climbed or otherwise risen to the top of the banking tree, but the tree is tall, and I lived as a child in a house with many stairs.

It was Perry Jesperson who came with me on my first visit to Pollaporra. He had borrowed one of his father's cars.

Even on the one-inch map, the topography was odd. It had struck me as odd many years before. I had always thought myself good with maps—as solitary children so often are—but now that I had been able to travel frequently, I had come to see that one cannot in every case divine from a map a feature of some kind that seems central when one actually arrives and inspects. In that way I had made a fool of myself on several occasions, though sometimes to my own knowledge only. When it comes to Scotland, I need hardly say that many one-inch maps are sometimes needed for a journey from one place to another, and that some of the maps depict little but heaving contours and huge hydroelectric installations.

Pollaporra stood isolated amid wild altitudes for miles around. Its loneliness was confirmed by its being marked at all. I knew very well that it was no Inveraray or even Balmoral. It stood about three and a half miles from the sea loch where Mason lived. That of course was as the crow flies, if crows there were. I had miled out the distance inaccurately with thumb and forefinger when I had still been a child. I had done it on many occasions. The topographical oddity was that the nearest depicted community was eight miles away in the opposite direction, whereas in such an area one would expect it to be on the sea, and to derive its hard living therefrom. It was difficult to think of any living at all for the place shown, which was stuck down in a hollow of the mountains, and was named Arrafergus. An uncoloured track was shown between Pollaporra and Arrafergus, the rough road of which I had heard so much, and along which my father's corse had passed a few years before. One could see the little cross marking the kirk and kirkyard where he lay. It was placed almost halfway between the two names, which seemed oddest of all. For much of the year, no congregation could assemble from either house or village. A footpath was shown between Pollaporra and the sea loch, but one could hardly believe in more than a technical right of way, perhaps initiated by smugglers and rebels.

I had commented upon all this to Jesperson before we left. He had said: "I expect it was an effect of the clearances."

"Or of the massacres," I had replied, not wishing to become involved in politics with Jesperson, even conversationally.

The roads were already becoming pretty objectionable, but Jesperson saw it all as progress, and we took it in turns to drive. On the third morning, we were advancing up the long road, yellow on the map, from the dead centre of Scotland to little Arrafergus. By English standards, it should not have been shown in yellow. Even Jesperson could hardly achieve more than a third of his normal speed. We had seen no other human being for a very long time, and even animals were absent, exactly as I had expected. Why was Arrafergus placed where it was, and how could it survive? Long ago, the soaking mist had compelled us to put up the hood of the roadster. I admit that it was April.

In the early afternoon, the road came to an end. We were in a deep cleft of the rock-strewn hills, and it would have been impossible for it to go further. There was a burn roaring, rather than gurgling, over the dark stones. There was no community, no place, not even a roadsign saying where we were or prohibiting further progress, not a shieling, not a crow. I speculated about what the funeral cortège could have done next.

"Do you want to get out and look for the foundations?" enquired Jesperson. "There's probably the odd stone to be found. The landlords razed everything, but I'm told there are usually traces."

"Not for the moment," I said. "Where do you suppose is the track to Pollaporra?"

"Up there," said Jesperson immediately, and pointed over my head.

How had I missed it? Despite the drizzle, I could now see it quite plainly. Nor must I, or anyone, exaggerate. The track was exceedingly steep and far from well metalled but, apart from the angle of incline, hardly worse to look at than the yellow road. Obviously, it must be difficult to keep the maps up to date, and in certain areas hardly worthwhile at present prices.

"Are we game?" I asked Jesperson. "It's not your car, and I don't want to press."

"We've got to spend the night somewhere," said Jesperson, who had not even stopped the engine.

After that all went surprisingly well. Cars were tougher and more flexible in those days. We ascended the mountain without once stopping, and there were no further major gradients until we came within sight of Pollaporra itself. I had feared that the track would die out altogether or become a desert of wiry weeds, such as spring up vengefully on modern roads, if for a moment neglected.

The little kirk was wrapped in rain which was now much heavier. There were a few early flowers amid and around the crumbling kirkyard walls. By June there would be more.

Jesperson drew up and this time stopped the engine reverently.

"It's all yours," he said, glancing at me sideways.

I stepped out. The huge new monument dominated the scene.

I scrambled across the fallen stones.

My father's full name was there, and his dates of birth and death. And then, in much smaller lettering, A JUST MAN A BRAVE MAN AND A GOOD. That was it: the commemorated was no-one's beloved husband or beloved father, nor were any of his honours specified, nor was confident hope expressed for him or, by implication, for anyone, he having been so admirable.

Around were memorials, large and small, to others among my unknown ancestors and collaterals; all far gone in chipping, flaking and greening or all that I studied. Among us we seemed to cram the entire consecrated area. Perhaps the residue from other families had no mementos. I was aware of the worms and maggots massed beneath my feet; crawling over one another, as in a natural history exhibit. At any moment, the crepe rubber soles of my shoes might crack and rot. Moreover, did the Church of Scotland ritually consecrate any place? I did not know. I turned round and realised that in the distance I could see Pollaporra also.

The house, though no more than a grey stone, slate-roofed rectangle, neither high nor particularly long, dominated the scene from then on, probably because it was the only work of man visible, apart from the bad road. Also it seemed to stand much higher than I had expected.

Jesperson wisely refused to set his father's car at the final ascent. We went up on foot. From the ridge we could make out the sea loch, green and phantasmal in the driving drizzle.

Cuddy was living in the house now, virtually pensioned off by the Trustees, and retained as caretaker—also as housekeeper, should the need arise, as it now did, almost certainly for the first time.

"Cuddy," I cried out in my best English university style, and with hand outstretched, as we entered. It was desirable to seem entirely confident.

"Brodick," she replied, not familiar perhaps, but independent.

"This is Mr Jesperson."

"It's too late for the shooting and too early for the fishing," said Cuddy. I think those were her words. I never quite remember the seasons.

"Mr Leith has come to take possession," said Perry Jesperson.

"It's his for his life," said Cuddy, as if indicating the duration of evening playtime.

"How *are* things?" I asked in my English university way. I was trying to ignore the chill, inner and outer, which the place cast.

"Wind and watertight as far as this house is concerned. You can inspect it at once. You'll not find one slate misplaced. For the rest you must ask Mr Mason."

"I shall do so tomorrow," I replied. "You must set me on the way to him."

"It is a straight road," said Cuddy. "You'll not go wrong."

Of course it was not a road at all, but a scramble over rocks and stones all three miles; slow, slippery and tiring. I could see why Mason spent little of his time visiting. None the less, the way was perfectly straight to the sea; though only from the top could one discern that. Jesperson had volunteered to look for some sport. Cuddy had been discouraging, but the house was as crammed with gear as the kirkyard with ancestral bones.

Mason lived in a small, single-storied house almost exactly at the end of the path, and at the edge of the sea. The local letter-box was in his grey wall, with a single collection at 6.30 a.m. each day, apart from Saturdays, Sundays and Public Holidays. There were a few other small houses, too small for the map but apparently occupied, and even a shop, with brooms in the window. The shop was now closed, and there was no indication of opening hours. A reasonably good, though narrow, road traversed the place, and in both directions disappeared along the edge of the loch. It ran between the path from Pollaporra and Mason's house. There was no detectable traffic, but there was a metal bus-stop sign, and a time table in a frame. I looked at it. If Jesperson's father's car were to break up, as seemed quite likely, we should need alternative transport. I saw that the bus appeared at 7 a.m. on the first Wednesday in each month between April and September. We had missed the April bus. I persisted and saw that the bus returned as early as 4.30 p.m. on the same day, and then went on to Tullochar at the head of the loch. Despite the length of the inlet, the waves were striking the narrow, stony beach sharply and rapidly. A few small and broken boats were lying about, and some meshes of sodden net, with shapeless cork floats. There was even a smell of dead crustaceans.

I realised that all these modest investigations were being observed by Mason himself. He had opened the faded brown door of his house and was standing there.

"Brodick Leith," he said, in the Scottish manner.

"Mr Mason," I replied. "I am very glad to meet you. I have heard about you all my life."

"Ay," said Mason, "you would have. Come indoors. We'll have a drop together and then I'll show you the books. I keep them to the day and hour. There's not as much to do as once there was."

"That was in my father's time?"

"In the Judge's time. Mr Justice Leith. Sir Roderic Leith, if you prefer. A strong man and a mysterious."

"I agree with what you say."

"Come inside," said Mason. "Come inside. I live as an unmarried man."

Mason opened a new bottle, and before I left, we had made our way through all of it, and had started on the remains of the previous one. Though I drank appreciably less than half, it was still, I think, more spirit than I had drunk on any previous occasion. The books were kept in lucid and impersonal handwriting, almost as good as my father's, and were flawless, in so far as I could understand them, my career in banking having not yet begun. Mason left me to go through them with the bottle at my elbow, while he went into the next room to cook us steaks, with his own hands. I could see for myself that the amounts brought out as surplus or profit at the end of each account were not large. I had never supposed they would be, but the costs and responsibilities of land ownership were brought home to me, none the less. Until then I had been a baby in the matter, as in many others. Most people are babies until they confront property ownership.

"I know you attended my father's funeral, Mr Mason," I said. "How was it? Tell me about it." The steak was proving to be the least prepared that I had ever attempted to munch. No doubt the cooking arrangements were very simple. I had not been invited to inspect them.

"Ay," said Mason, "and the funeral was the least of it." He took a heavier swig than before and stopped chewing altogether, while he thought.

"How many were there?" I had always been curious about that.

"Just me, and Cuddy MacFerrier, and the Shepstones."

The Shepstones were relatives. I had of course never set eyes upon even one of them. I had never seen a likeness. Millais had never painted a single Shepstone, and if one or more of them had appeared upon a criminal charge, my father would hardly have been the Judge.

"How many Shepstones?" I asked, still essaying to devour.

"Just the three of them," replied Mason, as if half-entranced. I am making little attempt to reproduce the Scottishness of his speech, or of anyone else's. I am far from being Sir Walter, or George Douglas.

"That is all there are?"

"Just the three. That's all," said Mason. "Drink up, man."

"A minister was there, of course?"

"Ay, the minister turned out for it. The son was sick, or so he said."

"I am the son," I said, smiling. "And I *was* sick. I promise you that."

"No need to promise anything," said Mason, still motionless. "Drink up, I tell you."

"And no-one else at all?" I persisted.

"Maybe the old carlin," said Mason. "Maybe her."

For me that was a very particular Scottish word. I had in fact sprung half to my feet, as Mason spoke it.

"Dinna fash yoursel'. She's gone awa' for the noo," said Mason.

He began once more to eat.

"I saw her once myself," I said, sitting right down again. "I saw her when my darling mother died."

"Ay, you would," said Mason. "Especially if maybe you were about the house at the time. Who let her in?"

"I don't know," I replied. "Perhaps she doesn't have to be let in?"

"Och, she does that," said Mason. "She always has to be let in."

"It was at the grave that you saw her?"

"No, not there, though it is my fancy that she was present. I saw her through that window as she came up from the sea."

I know that Mason pointed, and I know that I did not find it the moment to look.

"Through the glass panes or out on the wee rocks you can view the spot," said Mason. "It's always the same." Now he was looking at nothing and chewing vigorously.

"I saw no face," I said.

"If you'd seen that, you wouldn't be here now," said Mason. He was calm, as far as I could see.

"How often have you seen her yourself?"

"Four or five times in all. At the different deaths."

"Including at my mother's death?"

"Yes, then too," said Mason, still gazing upon the sawn-up sections of meat. "At the family deaths she is seen, and at the deaths of those, whoever they be, that enter the family."

I thought of my brother whom I had never known. I wasn't even aware that there had been any other family deaths during Mason's likely lifetime.

"She belongs to those called Leith, by one right or another," said Mason, "and to no-one at all else."

As he spoke, and having regard to the way he had put it, I felt that I saw why so apparently alert a man seemed to have such difficulty in remembering that I was presumably a Leith myself. I took his consideration kindly.

"I didn't see anyone when the Judge died," I remarked.

"Perhaps in a dream," said Mason. "I believe you were sick at the time."

That was not quite right of course, but it was true that I had by no means been in the house.

We dropped the subject, and turned once more to feu duties, rents and discriminatory taxes; even to the recent changes in the character of the tides and in the behaviour of the gannets.

I have no idea how I scrambled back to dismal Pollaporra, and in twilight first, soon in darkness. Perhaps the liquor aided instead of impeded, as liquor so often in practice does, despite the doctors and proctors.

III

After the War, Jack Oliver was there to welcome me back to the office off Cornhill. He was now a Colonel. His uncle had been killed in what was known as an incident, when the whole family house had been destroyed, including the Devises and De Wints. The business was now substantially his.

I found myself advanced very considerably from the position I had occupied in 1939. From this it is not to be supposed, as so many like to suppose, that no particular aptitude is required for success in merchant banking. On the contrary, very precise qualities both of mind and of temperament are needed. About myself, the conclusion I soon reached was that I was as truly a Scottish businessman as my ancestors in the kirkyard, whether I liked it or not, as O'Neill says. I should have been foolish had I *not* liked it. I might have preferred to be a weaver of dreams, but perhaps my mother had died too soon for that to be possible. I must add, however, that the business was by no means the same as when I had entered it before the War. No business was the same. The staff was smaller, the atmosphere tenser. The gains were illusory, the prospects shadowy. One worked much less hard, but one believed in nothing. There was little to work for, less to believe in.

It was in the office, though, that I met Shulie. She seemed very lost. I was attracted by her at once.

"Are you looking for someone?" I asked.

"I have just seen Mr Oliver." She had a lovely voice and a charming accent. I knew that Jack was seeking a new secretary. His present one had failed to report for weeks, or to answer her supposed home telephone number.

"I hope that all went well."

Shulie shook her head and smiled a little.

"I'm sorry about that."

"Mr Oliver had chosen a girl who went in just before me. It

always happens."

"I'm sure you'll have better luck soon."

She shook her head a second time. "I am not English."

"That has advantages as well as disadvantages," I replied firmly.

It struck me that she might be a refugee, with behind her a terrible story. She was small, slender and dark, though not as dark as my mother. I could not decide whether or not she looked particularly Jewish. I daresay it is always a rather foolish question.

"No advantages when you are in England," she said. "Can you please tell me how to get out of this place?"

"I'll come with you," I said. "It's difficult to explain."

That was perfectly true. It matters that it was true, because while we were winding through the corridors, and I was holding swing-doors, I was successful in persuading Shulie to have lunch with me. Time was gained for me also by the fact that Shulie had a slight limp, which slowed her down quite perceptibly. I am sure she was weary too, and I even believe that she was seriously underfed, whatever the exact reason. I perceived Shulie as a waif from the start; though also from the start I saw that it was far from the whole truth about her. I never learned the whole truth about her. Perhaps one never does learn, but Shulie refused, in so many words, to speak about it.

It was February, and outside I could have done with my overcoat. Jack Oliver still went everywhere in a British warm. He had several of them. There was snow on the ground and on the ledges. We had been under snow for weeks. Though do I imagine the snow? I do not imagine the cold. Shulie, when the blast struck her, drew into herself, as girls do. She was certainly not dressed for it; but few girls then were. The girlish image was still paramount. I myself actually caught a cold that day, as I often did. I was laid up for a time in my small flat off Orchard Street, and with no-one in any position to look after me very much. Later, Shulie explained to me that one need never catch cold. All that is necessary is a firm resolution against it—faith in oneself, I suppose.

On most days Jack and I, together or apart, went either to quite costly places or to certain pubs. That was the way of life approved, expected—even enforced—and, within the limits of the time, rewarded. I, however, had kept my options more open than that. I took Shulie to a nearby teashop, though a somewhat superior teashop. We were early, but it was filling fast. Still, we had a table to ourselves for a time.

"What's your name?"

"Shulie."

Her lips were like dark rose petals, as one imagines them, or sometimes dreams of them.

I have mentioned how lamentably sure I am that I failed to make Celia happy—nor any other girl. During the war, I had lived, off and on, with a woman married to another officer, who was never there when I was. I shall not relate how for me it all began. There was a case for, and a case against, but it had been another relationship inconducive to the ultimate happiness of either party.

When I realised that I was not merely attracted by Shulie, but deeply in love with her and dependent for any future I might have upon marrying her, I applied myself to avoiding past errors. Possibly in past circumstances, they had not really been errors; but now they might be the difference between life and death. I decided that, apart from my mother, I had never previously and properly loved anyone and that with no-one else but my mother had I been sufficiently honest to give things a chance. When the time came, I acted at once.

Within half an hour of Shulie tentatively accepting my proposal of marriage, I related to her what Mason had told me, and what I had myself seen. I said that I was a haunted man. I even said that she could reverse her tentative decision, if she thought fit.

"So the woman has to be let in?" said Shulie.

"That's what Mason told me."

"A woman who is married does not let any other woman in, except when her husband is not there."

"But suppose you were ill?"

"Then you would be at home looking after me. It would not be a time when you would let in another woman."

It was obvious that she was not taking the matter seriously. I had been honest, but I was still anxious.

"Have you ever heard a story like it before?"

"Yes," said Shulie. "But it is the message that matters more than the messenger."

After we married, Shulie simply moved in to my small flat. At first we intended or certainly I intended almost immediately to start looking for somewhere much larger. We—or certainly I—had a family in mind. With Shulie, I wanted that very much, even though I was a haunted man, whose rights were doubtful.

But it was amazing how well we seemed to go on living exactly where we were. Shulie had few possessions to bring in, and even when they were increased, we still seemed to have plenty of room. It struck me that Shulie's slight infirmity might contribute to her lack of interest in that normal ambition of any woman: a larger home. Certainly, the trouble seemed at times to fatigue her, even though the manifestations were very inconspicuous. For example, Jack Oliver, at a much later date, denied that he had ever noticed anything at all. The firm had provided me with a nice car and parking was then easier than it is now. Shulie had to do little walking of the kind that really exhausts a woman; pushing through crowds, and round shops at busy hours.

As a matter of fact, Shulie seldom left the flat, unless in my company. Shulie was writing a book. She ordered almost all goods on the telephone, and proved to be skilful and firm. She surprised me continually in matters like that. Marriage had already changed her considerably. She was plumper, as well as more confident. She accompanied me to the Festival Hall, and to picnics in Kew Gardens. The picnics were made elegant and exciting by her presence, and by her choice of what we ate and drank, and by the way she looked at the flowers, and by the way people and flowers looked at her. Otherwise, she wrote, or mused upon what she was about to write. She reclined in different sets of silk pyjamas on a bright blue daybed I'd bought for her, and rested her square, stiff-covered exercise book upon her updrawn knees. She refused to read to me what she had written, or to let me read it for myself. "You will know one day," she said.

I must admit that I had to do a certain amount of explaining to Jack Oliver. He would naturally have preferred me to marry a woman who kept open house and was equally good with all men alike. Fortunately, business in Britain does not yet depend so much upon those things as does business in America. I was able to tell Jack that setting a wife to attract business to her husband was always a chancy transaction for the husband. For better or for worse, Jack, having lately battled his way through a very complex divorce, accepted my view. The divorce had ended in a most unpleasant situation for Jack financially, as well as in some public ridicule. He was in no position even to hint that I had married a girl whom he had rejected for a job. His own wife had been the daughter of a baronet who was also a Vice-Admiral and a former Member of Parliament. Her name was Clarissa. Her mother, the Admiral's wife, was an M.F.H.

After my own mother's death, I should never have thought possible the happiness that Shulie released in me. There was much that remained unspoken to the end, but that may have been advantageous. Perhaps it is always so. Perhaps only madmen need to know everything and thus to destroy everything. When I lay in Shulie's arms, or simply regarded her as she wrote her secret book, I wished to know nothing more, because more would diminish. This state of being used to be known as connubial bliss. Few, I believe, experience it. It is certainly not a matter of deserts.

Shulie, however, proved to be incapable of conception. Possibly it was a consequence of earlier sufferings and endurances. Elaborate treatments might have been tried, but Shulie shrank from them, and understandably. She accepted the situation very quietly. She did not seem to cease loving me. We continued to dwell in the flat off Orchard Street.

I asked Shulie when her book would be finished. She replied that the more she wrote, the more there was to be written. Whenever I approached her, she closed the exercise book and lifted herself up to kiss me. If I persisted at all, she did more than kiss me.

I wanted nothing else in life than to be with Shulie, and alone with her. Everything we did in the outside world was incorporated into our love. I was happy once more, and now I was happy all the time, even in the office near Cornhill. I bought a bicycle to make the journey, but the City men laughed, and nicknamed me, and ragged me, so that Jack Oliver and the others suggested that I gave it up. Jack bought the bicycle himself, to use at his place in the country, where, not necessarily on the bicycle, he was courting the divorced daughter of the local High Sheriff, a girl far beyond his present means. She was even a member of a ladies' polo team, though the youngest. When one is happy oneself, everyone seems happy.

Our flat was on the top floor in a small block. The block had been built in more spacious days than the present, and there were two lifts. They were in parallel shafts. Above the waistline, the lifts had windows on three sides; the gate being on the fourth. They were large lifts, each "Licensed to carry 12 people"—far more than commonly accumulated at any one time. The users worked the lifts themselves though, when I had first taken the flat, the lifts in Selfridges round the corner had still been worked by the famous pretty girls in breeches, among whom an annual competition was held. The two lifts in the flats were brightly lit and always very clean. Shulie loved going up and down in them; much as she loved real traffic blocks, with boys ranging along the stationary cars selling ice-cream and evening newspapers. None the less, I do not think she used the lifts very much when I was not there. Travelling in them was, in fact, one tiny facet of our love. When Shulie was alone, I believe she commonly used the stairs, despite her trouble. The stairs were well lighted and well swept also. Marauders were seldom met.

Tenants used sometimes to wave to their neighbours through the glass, as the two lifts swept past one another, one upwards, one downwards. It was important to prevent this becoming a mere tiresome obligation. One morning I was alone in the descending lift. I was on my way to work: Bond Street underground station to Bank underground station. There had been a wonderful early morning with Shulie, and I was full of joy, thinking about nothing but that. The other lift swept upwards past me. In it were four people who lived in the flats: three women and one man, all known to me by sight, though no more than that. As a fifth, there was the woman whom I had seen when my mother died.

Despite the speed with which the lifts had passed, I was sure it was she. The back was turned to me, but her sparse hair, her dirty plaid, her stature and somehow her stance, were for ever unmistakable. I remember thinking immediately that the others in the lift must all be seeing the woman's face.

Melted ice flowed through me from the top of my head to the soles of my feet. There was a device for stopping the lift: "To be used only in Emergency". And of course I wanted to reverse the lift also. I was so cold and so shaky that I succeeded merely in jamming the lift, and neatly between floors, like a joke in "Puck" or "Rainbow", or a play by Sartre.

I hammered and raved, but most of the tenants had either

gone to work or were making preparations for coffee mornings. The other lift did not pass again. As many as ten minutes tore by before anyone took notice of me, and then it was only because our neighbour, Mrs Delmer, wanted to descend from the top, and needed the lift she always used, being, as she had several times told us, frightened of the other one. The caretaker emerged slowly from his cubicle and shouted to me that there was nothing he could do. He would have to send for the lift company's maintenance men. He was not supposed to be on duty at that hour anyway, he said. We all knew that. Mrs Delmer made a détour as she clambered down the staircase, in order to tap on the glass roof of my lift and give me a piece of her mind, though in refined phrases. In the end, I simply sank upon the floor and tried to close myself to all thought or feeling, though with no success.

I must acknowledge that the maintenance men came far sooner than one could have expected. They dropped from above, and crawled from below, even emerging from a trap in the lift floor, full of cheerful conversation, both particular and general. The lift was brought slowly down to the gate on the floor immediately below. For some reason, that gate would not open, even to the maintenance men; and we had to sink, slowly still, to the ground floor. The first thing I saw there was a liquid trail in from the street up to the gate of the other lift. Not being his hour, the caretaker had still to mop it up, even though it reeked of seabed mortality.

Shulie and I lived on the eighth floor. I ran all the way up. The horrible trail crossed our landing from the lift gate to under our front door.

I do not know how long I had been holding the key in my hand. As one does at such times, I fumbled and fumbled at the lock. When the door was open, I saw that the trail wound through the tiny hall or lobby and entered the living room. When the woman came to my mother, there had been a faint trail only, but at that time I had not learned from Mason about the woman coming from the sea. Fuller knowledge was yielding new evidence.

I did not find Shulie harmed, or ill, or dead. She was not there at all.

Everything was done, but I never saw her again.

IV

The trail of water soon dried out, leaving no mark of any kind, despite the rankness.

The four people whom I had seen in the lift, and who lived in the flats, denied that they had ever seen a fifth. I neither believed nor disbelieved.

Shulie's book was infinitely upsetting. It was hardly fiction at all, as I had supposed it to be, but a personal diary, in the closest detail, of everything we had done together, of everything we had been, of everything she had felt. It was at once comprehensive and chaste. At one time, I even thought of seeking a publisher for it, but was deterred, in an illogical way, by the uncertainty about what had happened to Shulie. I was aware that it had been perfectly possible for her to leave the building by the staircase, while I had been caged between floors in the lift. The staircase went down a shaft of its own.

The book contained nothing of what had happened to Shulie before she met me.

Shulie's last words were: "So joyful! Am I dreaming, or even dead? It seems that there is no external way of deciding either thing."

Presumably, she had then been interrupted. Doubtless, she had then risen to open the door.

I had been married to Shulie for three years and forty-one days.

I wrote to the Trustees suggesting that they put Pollaporra on the market, but their law agent replied that it was outside their powers. All I had done was upset both Cuddy and Mason.

I sold the lease of the flat off Orchard Street, and bought the lease of another one, off Gloucester Place.

I settled down to living with no-one and for no-one. I took every opportunity of travelling for the bank, no matter where—not only abroad, but even to Peterhead, Bolton or Camborne. Previously, I had not wished or cared to leave Shulie for a single night.

I pursued new delights, such as they were, and as they came along. I joined a bridge club, a chess club, a mahjong society, and a mixed fencing group. Later, I joined a very avant-garde dance club, and went there occasionally.

I was introduced by one of the people in my firm to a very High Anglican church in his own neighbourhood, and went there quite often. Sometimes I read one of the lessons. I was one of the few who could still do that in Latin.

Another partner was interested in masonics, but I thought that would be inconsistent. I did join a livery company: it is expected in the City.

I was pressed to go in for regular massage, but resisted that too.

I was making more paper money than I would ever have thought possible. Paper money? Not even that. Phantom wealth, almost entirely: taxes took virtually the whole of it. I did not even employ a housekeeper. I did not wish for the attentions of any woman who was not Shulie. All the same, I wrote to Celia, who replied at once, making clear, among very many other things, that she was still unmarried. She had time to write so long and so prompt a letter. She had hope enough to think it worthwhile.

It is amazing how full a life a man can lead without for one moment being alive at all, except sometimes when sleeping. As Clifford Bax says, life is best treated as simply a game. Soon enough one will be bowled middle stump, be put out of action in the scrum, or ruled offside and sent off. As Bax also says, it is necessary to have an alternative. But who really has?

None the less, blood will out, and I married again. Sometime before, Shulie's death had been "presumed". Mercifully, it was the Trustees who attended to that.

I married Clarissa. I am married to her now.

The court had bestowed upon Clarissa a goodly slice of Jack's property and prospects, and Jack was recognised by all as having made a complete fool of himself, not only in the area of cash; but Clarissa never really left at all. Even though Jack was now deeply entangled with Suzanne, herself a young divorcée, Clarissa was always one of Jack's house party, eager to hear everything, ready to advise, perhaps even to comfort, though I myself never came upon her doing that. She might now be sleeping in the room that had once been set aside for the visits of her sister, Naomi, but of course she knew the whole house far more intimately than Jack did, or than any normal male knows any house. She continued being invaluable to Jack; especially when he was giving so much of his time to Suzanne. One could not know Jack at all well, let alone as well as I knew him, without continuing to encounter Clarissa all the time.

The word for Clarissa might be deft—the first word, that is. She can manage a man or a woman, a slow child or a slow pensioner, as effortlessly as she can manage everything in a house, at a party, in a shop, on a ship. She has the small but right touch for every single situation—the perfect touch. Most of all, she has the small and perfect touch for every situation, huge or tiny, in her own life. Few indeed have *that* gift. No doubt Clarissa owes much to her versatile papa. On one occasion also, I witnessed Clarissa's mother looking after a difficult meet. It was something to note and remember.

Clarissa has that true beauty which is not so much in the features and body, but around them: nothing less than a mystical emanation. When I made my proposal to Clarissa, I naturally thought very devoutly of Shulie. Shulie's beauty was of the order one longs from the first to embrace, to be absorbed by.

Of course, my mother's dark beauty had been like that also. Clarissa one hardly wished or dared to touch, lest the vision fade. A man who felt otherwise than that about Clarissa, would be a man who could not see the vision at all. I imagine that state of things will bear closely upon what happens to Clarissa. There is little that is mystical about Clarissa's detectable behaviour, though there must be *some* relationship between her soul and the way she looks. It is a question that arises so often when women as beautiful as Clarissa materialise in one's rose garden. I myself have never seen another woman as beautiful absolutely as Clarissa, or certainly never spoken to one.

Clarissa has eyes so deep as to make one wonder about the whole idea of depth, and what it means. She has a voice almost as lovely as her face. She has a slow and languorous walk, beautiful too, but related, I fear, to an incident during her early teens, when she broke both legs in the hunting field. Sometimes it leads to trouble when Clarissa is driving a car. Not often. Clarissa prefers to wear trousers, though she looks perfectly normal in even a short skirt, indeed divinely beautiful, as always.

I fear that too much of my life with Clarissa has been given to quarrelling. No-one is to blame, of course.

There was a certain stress even at the proposal scene, which took place on a Saturday afternoon in Jack's house, when the others were out shooting duck. Pollaporra and its legend have always discouraged me from field sports, and all the struggling about had discouraged Clarissa, who sat before the fire, looking gnomic.

But she said Yes at once, and nodded, and smiled.

Devoted still, whether wisely or foolishly, to honesty, I told her what Mason had told me, and what I had myself seen on two occasions, and that I was a haunted man.

Clarissa looked very hostile. "I don't believe in things like that," she said sharply.

"I thought I ought to tell you."

"Why? Did you want to upset me?"

"Of course not. I love you. I don't want you to accept me on false pretences."

"It's got nothing to do with my accepting you. I just don't want to know about such things. They don't exist."

"But they do, Clarissa. They are part of me."

From one point of view, obviously I should not have persisted. I had long recognised that many people would have said that I was obsessed. But the whole business seemed to me the explanation of my being. Clarissa must not take me to be merely a banker, a youngish widower, a friend of her first husband's, a faint simulacrum of the Admiral.

Clarissa actually picked up a book of sweepstake tickets and threw it at me as I sat on the rug at her feet.

"There," she said.

It was a quite thick and heavy book, but I was not exactly injured by it, though it had come unexpectedly, and had grazed my eye.

Clarissa then leaned forward and gave me a slow and searching kiss. It was the first time we had kissed so seriously.

"There," she said again.

She then picked the sweepstake tickets off the floor and threw them in the fire. They were less than fully burnt ten minutes later, when Clarissa and I were more intimately involved, and looking at our watches to decide when the others were likely to return.

The honeymoon, at Clarissa's petition, was in North Africa, now riddled with politics, which I did not care for. For centuries, there has been very little in North Africa for an outsider to see, and the conformity demanded by an alien society seemed not the best background for learning to know another person. Perhaps we should have tried Egypt, but Clarissa specifically demanded something more rugged. With Shulie there had been no honeymoon.

Before marrying me, Clarissa had been dividing her life between her flat and Jack's country house. Her spacious flat, very near my childhood home, was in its own way as beautiful as she was, and emitted a like glow. It would have been absurd for me not to move into it. The settlement from Jack had contributed significantly to all around me, but by now I was able to keep up, or nearly so. Money is like sex. The more that everyone around is talking of little else, the less it really accounts for, let alone assists.

Not that sex has ever been other than a problem with Clarissa. I have good reason to believe that others have found the same, though Jack never gave me one word of warning. In any case, his Suzanne is another of the same kind, if I am any judge; though less beautiful, and, I should say, less kind also. Men chase the same woman again and again—or rather the same illusion—or rather the same lost part of themselves.

Within myself, I had of course returned to the hope of children. Some will say that I was a fool not to have had that matter out with Clarissa before marrying her, and no doubt a number of related matters also. They speak without knowing Clarissa. No advance terms can be set. None at all. I doubt whether it is possible with any woman whom one finds really desirable. Nor can the proposal scene be converted into a businesslike discussion of future policy and prospects. That is not the atmosphere, and few would marry if it were.

With Shulie, the whole thing had been love. With Clarissa, it was power—and she was so accustomed to the power being hers that she could no longer bother to exercise it, except indirectly. This was and is true even though Clarissa is exceedingly good-hearted in many other ways. I had myself experienced something of the kind in reverse with poor Celia, though obviously in a much lesser degree.

Clarissa has long been impervious to argument or importunity or persuasion of any kind. She is perfectly equipped with counterpoise and equipoise. She makes discussion seem absurd. Almost always it is. Before long, I was asking myself whether Clarissa's strange and radiant beauty was compatible with desire, either on her part or on mine.

There was also the small matter of Clarissa's black maid, Aline, who has played her little part in the immediate situation. On my visits to the flat before our marriage, I had become very much aware of Aline, miniature and slender, always in tight sweater and pale trousers. Clarissa had told me that Aline could do everything in the place that required to be done, but in my hearing Aline spoke little for herself. I was told that often she drove Clarissa's beautiful foreign car, a present from Jack less than a year before the divorce. I was also told, as a matter of interest, that Jack had never met Aline. I therefore never spoke of her to him. I was telling him much less now in any case. I certainly did not tell him what I had not previously been told myself: that when I was away for the firm, which continued to be frequently, Aline took my place in Clarissa's vast and swan-like double bed. I discovered this in a thoroughly low way, which I do not propose to relate. Clarissa simply remarked to me that, as I knew, she could never sleep well if alone in the room. I abstained from rejoining that what Clarissa really wanted was a nanny; one of those special nannies who, like dolls, are always there to be dominated by their charges. It would have been one possible rejoinder.

Nannies were on my mind. It had been just then that the Trustees wrote to me about Cuddy. They told me that Cuddy had "intimated a wish" to leave her employment at Pollaporra. She wanted to join her younger sister, who, I was aware, had a business on the main road, weaving and plaiting for the tourists, not far from Dingwall. I could well believe that the business had become more prosperous than when I had heard about it as a child. It was a business of the sort that at the moment did. The Trustees went on to imply that it was my task, and not theirs, to find a successor to Cuddy. They reminded me that I was under an obligation to maintain a property in which I had merely a life interest.

It was a very hot day. Clarissa always brought the sun. She had been reading the letter over my shoulder. I was always aware of her special nimbus encircling my head and torso when she did this. Moreover, she was wearing nothing but her nightdress.

"Let's go and have a look," she said.

"Are you sure you want to?" I asked, remembering her response to my story.

"Of course I'm sure. I'll transform the place, now I've got it to myself."

"That'll be the day," I said, smiling up at her.

"You won't know it when I've finished with it. Then we can sell it."

"We can't," I said. "Remember it's not mine to sell."

"You must get advice. Jack might be able to help."

"You don't know what Pollaporra's like. Everything is bound to be totally run down."

"With your Cuddy in charge all these years, and with nothing else to do with herself? At least, you say not."

I had seen on my previous visit that this argument might be sound, as far as it went.

"You can't possibly take on all the work."

"We'll have Aline with us. I had intended that."

By now, I had seen for myself also that Aline was indeed most competent and industrious. It would have been impossible to argue further: Clarissa was my wife and had a right both to accompany me and to take someone with her to help with the chores. If I were to predecease her, she would have a life interest in the property. Moreover, Clarissa alone could manage very well for us when she applied herself. I had learned that too. There were no sensible, practical objections whatever.

"Aline will be a help with the driving as well," added Clarissa.

There again, I had seen for myself how excellent a driver

little Aline could be. She belongs to just the sort of quiet person who in practice drives most effectively on the roads of today.

"So write at once and say we're arriving," said Clarissa.

"I'm not sure there's anyone to write to," I replied. "That's the point."

I had, of course, a set of keys. For whatever reason, I did not incline to giving Mason advance notice of my second coming, and in such altered circumstances.

"I'm not sure how Aline will get on with the Highlanders," I remarked. There are, of course, all those stories in Scotland about the intrusion of huge black men, and sometimes, I fancy, of black females. They figure in folk lore everywhere.

"She'll wind each of them three times round each of her fingers," replied Clarissa. "But you told me there *were* no Highlanders at Pollaporra."

Clarissa, when triumphing, looked like Juno, or Diana, or even Minerva.

Aline entered to the tinkling of a little bell. It is a pretty little bell, which I bought for Clarissa in Sfax, her earlier little bell having dropped its clapper. When Aline entered in her quiet way, Clarissa kissed her, as she does every morning upon first sighting Aline.

"We're all three going into the wilderness together," said Clarissa. "Probably on Friday."

Friday was the day after tomorrow. I really could not leave the business for possibly a week at such short notice. There was some tension because of that, but it could not be helped.

When we did reach Pollaporra, the weather was hotter than ever, though there had been several thunderstorms in London. Aline was in her element. Clarissa had stocked up the large car with food in immense quantity. When we passed through an outlying area of Glasgow, she distributed two pounds of sweets to children playing in the roads of a council estate. The sweets were melting in their papers as she threw them. The tiny fingers locked together.

When we reached the small kirkyard Clarissa, who was driving us along the rough road from Arrafergus, categorically refused to stop.

"We're here to drive the bogies out," she said, "not to let them in."

Clarissa also refused to leave the car at the bottom of the final slope, as Perry Jesperson had done. My friend Jesperson was now a Labour M.P. like his father, and already a Joint Parliamentary Secretary and much else vaguely lucrative and responsible. Clarissa took the car up the very steep incline as if it had been a lift at the seaside.

She stood looking at and beyond the low grey house. "Is that the sea?" she asked, pointing.

"It's the sea loch," I replied. "A long inlet, like a fjord."

"It's a lovely place," said Clarissa.

I was surprised, but, I suppose, pleased.

"I thought we might cut the house up into lodges for the shooting and fishing," said Clarissa. "But now I don't want to."

"The Trustees would never have agreed," I pointed out. "They have no power to agree."

"Doesn't matter. I want to come here often. Let's take a photograph."

So, before we started to unpack the car, Clarissa took one of Aline and me; and, at her suggestion, I took one of Aline and her. Aline did not rise to the shoulders of either of us.

Within the house, the slight clamminess of my previous visit had been replaced by a curiously tense airlessness. I had used my key to admit us, but I had not been certain as to whether or not Cuddy was already gone, and Clarissa and I went from room to room shouting for her, Clarissa more loudly than I. Aline remained among the waders and antlers of the entrance hall, far from home and thinking her own thoughts. There was no reply anywhere. I went to the door of what I knew to be Cuddy's own room, and quietly tapped. When there was no reply there either, I gently tried the handle. I thought the door might be locked, but it was not. Inside was a small unoccupied bedroom. The fittings were very spare. There were a number of small framed statements on the walls, such as "I bow before Thee", and "Naught but Surrender", and "Who knows All", without a mark of interrogation. Clarissa was still calling from room to room. I did not care to call back, but went after her on half-tiptoe.

I thought we could conclude we were alone. Cuddy must have departed some time ago.

Dust was settling everywhere, even in that remote spot. The sunlight made it look like encroaching fur. Clarissa seemed undeterred and undaunted.

"It's a lost world and I'm queen," she said.

It is true that old grey waders, and wicker fish baskets with many of the withies broken, and expensive guns for stalking lined up in racks, are unequalled for suggesting loss, past, present and to come. Even the pictures were all of death and yesterday; stags exaggeratedly virile before the crack shot, feathers abnormally bright before the battue, men and ancestors in bonnets before, behind and around the ornamentally piled carcases, with the lion of Scotland flag stuck in the summit. When we reached the hall, I noticed that Aline was shuddering in the sunlight. I myself had never been in the house before without Cuddy. In practice, she had been responsible for everything that happened there. Now I was responsible—and for as long as I remained alive.

"We'll paint everything white and we'll put in a swimming pool," cried Clarissa joyously. "Aline can have the room in the tower."

"I didn't know there was a tower," I said.

"*Almost* a tower," said Clarissa.

"Is there anything in the room?" I asked.

"Only those things on heads. They're all over the walls and floor."

At that, Aline actually gave a little cry. Perhaps she was

thinking of things on walls and floors in Africa.

"It's all right," said Clarissa, going over to her. "We'll throw them all away. I promise. I never ask you to do anything I don't do myself, or wouldn't do."

But, whatever might be wrong, Aline was uncomforted. "Look!" she cried, and pointed out through one of the hall windows, all of them obstructed by stuffed birds in glass domes, huge and dusty.

"What have you seen this time?" asked Clarissa, as if speaking to a loved though exhausting child.

At that moment, it came to me that Clarissa regularly treated Aline as my mother had treated me.

Aline's hand fell slowly to her side, and her head began to droop.

"It's only the car," said Clarissa. "*Our* car. You've been driving it yourself."

I had stepped swiftly but quietly behind the two of them. I admit that I too could see nothing but the car and, of course, the whole of Scotland.

I seldom spoke directly to Aline, but now was the moment.

"What was it?" I asked, as sympathetically as I could manage. "What did you see?"

But Aline had begun to weep, as by now I had observed that she often did. She wept without noise or any special movement. The tears just flowed like thawing snow: as they do in nature, though less often on change.

"It was nothing," said Clarissa. "Aline often sees nothing, don't you, Aline?" She produced her own handkerchief, and began to dry Aline's face, and to hug her tightly.

The handkerchief was from an enormous casket of objects given us as a wedding present by Clarissa's grandmother (on the mother's side), who was an invalid, living in Dominica. Clarissa's grandfather had been shot dead years before by thieves he had interrupted.

"Now," said Clarissa after a few moments of tender reassurance. "Smile, please. That's better. We're going to be happy here, one and all. Remember. Happy."

I suppose I was reasonably eager, but I found it difficult to see how she was going to manage it. It was not, as I must in justice to her make clear, that normally I was unhappy with Clarissa. She was too beautiful and original for that to be the word at any time. The immediate trouble was just Pollaporra itself: the most burdensome and most futile of houses, so futile as to be sinister, even apart from its associations, where I was concerned. I could not imagine any effective brightening; not even by means of maquillage and disguise: a pool, a discothéque, a sauna, a black-jack suite. To me Pollaporra was a millstone I could never throw away. I could not believe that modern tenants would ever stop there for long, or in the end show us a profit. For all the keep-nets and carcase-sleighs in every room, I doubted whether the accessible sport was good enough to be marketed at all in contemporary terms. Nor had I started out with Clarissa in order that we should settle down in the place ourselves. When I can get away from work, I want somewhere recuperative. About Pollaporra, I asked the question all married couples ask when detached from duties and tasks: what should we do all day? There was nothing.

"I have never felt so free and blithe," said Clarissa later that evening, exaggerating characteristically but charmingly. She was playing the major part in preparing a quite elaborate dinner for us out of tins and packets. In the flat, Aline had normally eaten in her own pretty sitting-room, but here she would be eating with us. Clarissa would be tying a lace napkin round her neck, and heaping her plate with first choices, and handing her date after date on a spike. Employees are supposed to be happier when treated in that way, though few people think it is true, and few employees.

"We'll flatten the roof and have li-los," said Clarissa, while Aline munched with both eyes on her plate, and I confined myself to wary nibblings round the fringe of Rognons Turbigo, canned but re-invigorated. The plates at Pollaporra depicted famous Scots, such as Sawney Bean and Robert Knox, who employed Burke and Hare, the body-snatchers. Mr Justice Leith, who despised the criminal law, had never been above such likenesses, as we know—nor had he been the only sporting jurist in the family, very far from it.

"I think to do that we'd have to rebuild the house," I remarked.

"Do try not to make difficulties the whole time. Let yourself go, Brodick."

It is seldom a good idea, according to my experience, and especially not in Scotland, but of course I could see what Clarissa meant. There was no reason why we should not make of the trip as much of a holiday as was possible. It would be a perfectly sensible thing to do. If Clarissa was capable of fun at Pollaporra, I was the last person with a right to stand in her way.

"We might build a gazebo," I said, though I could feel my heart sinking as I spoke.

Aline, with her mouth full of prunes (that day), turned her head towards me. She did not know what a gazebo was.

"A sort of summer house," explained Clarissa. "With cushions and views. It would be lovely. So many things to look at."

I had never known Clarissa so simple-minded before; in the nicest sense, of course. I realised that this might be a Clarissa more real than the other one. I might have to consider where I myself stood about that. On the other hand, Pollaporra instead of bringing out at long last the real woman, might be acting upon her by contraries, and have engaged the perversity in her, and to no ultimately constructive end. I had certainly heard of that too, and in my time seen it in action among friends.

"I don't want to look," said Aline, expelling prune-stones into spoons.

"You will by tomorrow. You'll feel quite different. We're going to drive all the banshees far, far away."

I am sure that Aline did not know what a banshee was either, but Clarissa's general meaning was clear, and the word has an African, self-speaking sound in itself, when one comes to think about it. Words for things like that are frightening in themselves the world over.

Only Clarissa, who believed in nothing she could not see or imagine, was utterly undisturbed. I am sure that must have played its part in the row we had in our room that night.

There were small single rooms, of course, several of them. There were also low dormitories for body servants and sporting auxiliaries. All the rooms for two people had Scottish double beds. Clarissa and I had to labour away in silence making such a bed with sheets she had brought with us. Blankets we should have had to find in drawers and to take on trust, but on such a night they were unnecessary. Aline, when not with Clarissa, always slept in a striped bag, which that night must have been far too hot. Everything, everywhere, was far too hot. That contributed too, as it always does. Look at Latin America!

I admit that throughout the evening I had failed to respond very affirmatively to Clarissa's sequence of suggestions for livening up the property and also (she claimed) increasing its market value; which, indeed, cannot, as things were and are, be high. I could see for myself how I was leading her first into despondancy, then into irritation. I can see that only too well now. I was dismayed by what was happening, but there was so little I could conscientiously offer in the way of encouragement. All I wished to do with Pollaporra was patch up some arrangement to meet my minimum obligations as a life tenant, and then, if possible, never set eyes upon the place again. One reason why I was cast down was the difficulty of achieving even a programme as basic as that. I daresay that Clarissa's wild ideas would actually be simpler to accomplish, and conceivably cheaper also in the end. But there is something more than reason that casts me down at Pollaporra. Shall I say that the house brings into consciousness the conflict between my hereditament and my identity? Scotland herself is a land I do well to avoid.

Many of us have large areas of danger which others find merely delightful.

There was no open row until Clarissa and I went upstairs. One reason was that after doing the washing-up, Aline had come into the sitting-room, without a word, to join us. I was not surprised that she had no wish to be alone—nor that she proved reluctant to play a game named Contango, of which Clarissa was very fond, and which went back to her days with Jack, even though Jack had always won, sometimes while glancing through business papers simultaneously, as I had observed for myself. Both Clarissa and Aline were wearing tartan trousers, though not the same tartan. I had always been told by Cuddy that there was no Leith tartan. I have never sought further to know whether or not that is true.

As soon as we were in bed, Clarissa lay on her front, impressing the pillow with moisture from her brow, and quietly set about me, ranging far beyond the possibilities and deficiencies of Pollaporra. Any man—any modern man—would have some idea of what was said. Do the details matter? I offered no argument. At Pollaporra, I spoke as little as I could. What can argument achieve anywhere? It might have been a moment for me to establish at least temporary dominance by one means or another, but Pollaporra prevented, even if I am the man to do it at any time. I tried to remember Shulie, but of course the circumstances left her entirely unreal to me, together with everything else.

And, in the morning, things were no better. I do not know how much either of us had managed to sleep. For better or worse, we had fallen silent in the heat long ago. In the end, I heard the sea birds screaming and yelling at the dawn.

Clarissa put on a few garments while I lay silent on the bed and then told me that as there was nothing she could do in the house, she was departing at once.

"I should leave Aline behind, but I need her."

"I quite understand," I said. "I advised you against coming

in the first place. I shall go over to see Mason and try to arrange with him for a caretaker. It won't take more than a day or two."

"You'll first need to change the place completely. You are both weak and pigheaded."

"They sometimes see things differently in Scotland. I shall come down as soon as I can." I might have to hire a car to some station, because I did not think Mason owned one, or anyone else in his small community. That was a trifle; comparatively.

"No hurry. I shall use the time deciding what to do for the best." She was combing her mass of hair, lovely as Ceres' sheaf. The comb, given her by the Aga Khan, was made of ebony. The air smelled of hot salt.

I suppose I should have begged her pardon for Pollaporra and myself, and gone back to London with her, or to anywhere else. I did not really think of it. Pollaporra had to be settled, if at all possible. I might never be back there.

In a few moments, Clarissa and I were together in the hall, the one high room, and I saw Aline silently standing by the outer door, as if she had stood all night; and the door was slightly open. Aline was in different trousers, and so was Clarissa.

"I can't be bothered to pack up the food. You're welcome to all of it."

"Don't go without breakfast," I said. "The lumpy roads will make you sick."

"Breakfast would make me sick," said Clarissa.

Clarissa carried very few clothes about. All she had with her was in the aircraft holdall she clutched. I do not know about Aline. She must have had something. I cannot remember.

"I don't know when we'll meet again," said Clarissa.

"In two or three days," I said. "Four at the most." Since I had decided to remain, I had to seem calm.

"I may go and stay with Naomi. I want to think things out."

She was wearing the lightest of blouses, little more than a mist. She was exquisite beyond description. Suddenly, I noticed that tears were again streaming silently down Aline's face.

"Or I may go somewhere else," said Clarissa, and walked out, with her slight but distinctive wobble.

Instead of immediately following her, as she always did, Aline actually took two steps in my direction. She looked up at me, like a Rococo cherub. Since I could not kiss Clarissa, I lightly kissed Aline's wet lips, and she kissed me.

I turned my back in order not to see the car actually depart, though nothing could prevent my hearing it. What had the row been really about? I could surmise and guess, but I did not know. I much doubted whether Clarissa knew. One could only be certain that she would explain herself, as it were to a third party, in a totally different way from me. We might just as well belong to different zoological species, as in the Ray Bradbury story. The row was probably a matter only of Clarissa being a woman and I a man. Most or all rows between the sexes have no more precise origin—and, indirectly, many other rows also.

I think I stood for some time with my back to the open door and my face to the picture of an old gillie in a tam, with dead animals almost to his knees. It had been given us by the Shepstones. It was named "Coronach" in Ruskinian letters, grimly misapplied. Ultimately, I turned and through the open door saw what Aline may have seen. The auld carlin was advancing across the drive with a view to entering.

Drive, I have to call it. It was a large area of discoloured nothingness upon which cars stood, and before them horses, but little grew, despite the lack of weeding. Needless to say, the woman was not approaching straightforwardly. Previously, I had seen her only when she had been confined to the limits of a staircase, albeit a wide one, a landing, and, later, a lift. If now she had been coming straight at me, I might have had a split second to see her face. I realised that, quite clearly, upon the instant.

I bounded forward. I slammed the door. The big key was

difficult to turn in the big lock, so I shot the four rusty bolts first. Absurdly, there was a chain also and, after I had coped with the stiff lock, I put it on.

Then I tore round the house shooting other bolts; making sure that all other locks were secure; shutting every possible window and aperture, on that already very hot early morning.

It is amazing how much food Clarissa laid in. She was, or is, always open-handed. I am sure that I have made that clear. Nor of course does one need so much food—or as least want so much—in this intense heat. Nor as yet has the well run dry. Cuddy refused to show me the well, saying the key was lost. I have still not seen either thing.

There is little else to do but write this clear explanation of everything that has happened to me since the misfortune of birth. He that has fared better, and without deceiving himself, let him utter his jackass cry.

Not that I have surrendered. There lies the point. Pollaporra is not on the telephone, nor ever could be, pending the "withering away of the State"; but before long someone may take note that I am not there. The marines may descend from choppers yet. Clarissa may well have second thoughts. Women commonly do, when left to themselves. She loves Pollaporra and may well devise a means of wresting my life-interest away from me, and welcome. I don't know where Aline would enter into that hypothesis. Possibly I made a mistake in not writing to Mason that I was coming. But I doubt whether in such personal matters his time-scale is shorter than months.

Off and on, I see the woman at one window or another; though not peeking through, which, as will have been gathered, is far from her policy. At least twice, however, it has been at a window upstairs; on both occasions when I was about to undress for some reason, not necessarily slumber, of which I have little. At these times, her slimy-sleek head, always faceless, will tip-tap sharply against the thick glazing bars. The indelicacy, as

Jack might put it (I wonder how Cuddy would put it?), set me upon a course of hard thinking.

So long as I keep myself barred up, she can achieve nothing. Mason seemed quite certain of that, and I accept it. But what does the woman aim to do to me? When she appeared to me before, my poor mother soon passed away. When she appeared to me a second time, my dear, dear Shulie vanished from my life. It is not to be taken for granted that either of these precise fates is intended for me. I am not even ill or infirm. There may be a certain room for manoeuvre, though I can foresee no details.

More often, I see the woman at corners of what used to be the lawn and garden, though never in my time. It lies at the back of the house, and far below lies the loch. Sometimes too, the creature perches on the ornaments and broken walls, like a sprite. Such levitations are said to be not uncommon in the remoter parts of Scotland. Once I thought I glimpsed her high up in a bush, like dirty rags in a gale. Not that so far there has been any gale, or even any wind. The total silent stillness is one of the worst things. If I die of heat and deoxygenation, it will be one solution.

Yes, it is a battle with strong and unknown forces that I have on my hands. "But what can ail all of them to bury the old carlin in the night time?" as Sir Walter ventures to enquire; in "The Antiquary", if I remember rightly.